Point of Origin

Book Three
Tru Exceptions Series

WRITTEN BY
Amanda Tru

Point of Origin
Copyright © 2012 by Amanda Tru

Cover design by Samantha Bayarr

Walker Hammond Publishers
ISBN-13: 978-0615674131 (Custom)
ISBN-10: 0615674135
Also available in ebook publication

PRINTED IN THE UNITED STATES OF AMERICA

Chapter 1

The crunch of leaves and twigs under the horse's hooves sounded loud in the hushed canopy of the forest. She had to be getting close. Cautiously, Rachel urged her horse, Roosevelt, through the brush.

Something wasn't right.

Intermixed with the refreshing scent of pine and foliage was a hint of something else Rachel couldn't identify. It had a faint, almost chemical bite to it.

Rachel ignored the tickle of foreboding slowly crawling up her spine. She was not going to turn back now. That strange light had come from somewhere right around here. Rachel was sure of it.

From the ridge overlooking this little valley, she had seen a light flicker in the afternoon glare as if a sunbeam had been captured by a mirror and reflected in one brief, intense flash. It was over before Rachel could be sure of what she had seen.

But she hadn't imagined it. Something had caused that flash, and she was going to figure out what.

It was dark beneath the thick trees and brush. It was so still, she could hear her own heartbeat.

Why was she suddenly so nervous?

I shouldn't be here alone!

But that was ridiculous! This was her family's ranch. Sure, there wasn't another person for at least a couple miles in any direction, but she had spent her entire life on this vast property. There wasn't anything around here that she couldn't handle herself.

There! Her eyes caught sight of something peeking through the trees. It looked like part of a roof. But that was impossible! There couldn't be a house here on their property! She carefully maneuvered to get a better look. It was definitely the roof of some structure. Could it be squatters? Rachel nervously put her hand on the Winchester 30-30 strapped to the saddle. She had left her smaller weapons at home, thinking a rifle would be more practical for this trip. Now she was regretting her decision.

She nervously urged the horse forward, the rest of the building now coming into view. It was a rough-hewn cabin, more like a shack. The metal roofing had been covered with some sort of dark material. But, Rachel saw that part of the material had slipped, revealing a section of bright, reflective metal. That section catching the rays of the sun must have been what she had seen from the ridge.

Rachel slid from her saddle to the ground, taking the rifle with her. She loosely tied Roosevelt's reins to a tree, confident that the big bay stallion would stay until she returned. He was one of their best horses, her dad's favorite. He wouldn't leave without her.

She moved forward, placing her weight on the balls of her feet and keeping her footfalls silent. There were no signs of life as she approached the shack. It actually seemed like a solidly built structure; it just wasn't pretty. The outside was bare, rough timber thrown together in a seemingly haphazard fashion. There were a few windows, but they were high and seemed more for ventilation than decoration.

That sense of foreboding was now suffocating, encompassing Rachel like a shroud as she reached the door. Standing on her tiptoes, she peered inside the window to the right. The place appeared empty.

Rachel put her hand on the doorknob and turned. It was unlocked, opening soundlessly.

The second she stepped inside, she knew she'd made a mistake.

Diagrams and maps covered the walls. Strange containers and equipment lay on tables around the room. Three computers waited in a line against the long wall to her left. It looked like some kind of combination laboratory and workshop. Rachel didn't know what she'd walked into, but she saw enough to know she was way over her head.

She heard voices coming from the opposite side of the building. Rachel backed out the door. She had to get out of here fast. Whatever these people were doing, they weren't going to be happy about having visitors.

She spun, intending to sprint to her horse, but her foot caught a metal bucket by the door, sending it banging loudly across the wood floor. Rachel frantically glanced over her shoulder, seeing the door on the opposite side start to open and hearing sudden shouting over the clanging metal.

She didn't wait to see who opened the door. She ran.

Reaching Roosevelt, she placed her boot into the stirrup, heaved herself into the saddle, and urged him into a full gallop. Trees blurred as she raced through the forest.

What had she done?

Her thoughts swirled in a confusing mess. Escape was the only coherent, driving force. Her heartbeat kept pace with the horse's rapid hooves pounding the ground. Her breathing came in shudders. Had she been seen?

They had to slow as they reached the steep wall of the valley.

Any hope of not being followed was shattered with the first gunshot.

Rachel bent low over the horse, feeling exposed as they climbed. She tried to direct Roosevelt on a route using the trees as cover, but the foliage was more sparse on the steep rise. The horse's hooves slid on the crumbling rock and dirt, struggling to find adequate footing.

Her rifle sat clutched in her lap, but she dare not take the time to return fire. Besides, she had no idea how many were after her. If there had been another way out of the valley, Rachel would have taken it, but this was still the most direct route to get help.

Shots echoed above her again and again, chilling in their hollow sound. But she didn't pause.

God, get me out of here! she prayed as she clutched tightly to the horse and willed him forward.

Finally, small rocks spun off below as the horse's hooves grabbed the top of the ridge. But Rachel felt little relief as they left the valley behind and galloped across the plain. She now realized that she had seen something she shouldn't—something dangerous. There was no way her pursuers would let her go so easily. There was no way they would let her go alive.

Chapter 2

At least the gunshots seemed to stop after she made it over the ridge. Trying to take advantage of the level terrain, Rachel pushed Roosevelt as fast as he could go, making a beeline for the ranch. After about five minutes at the breakneck pace, Rachel pulled the horse back as reason prevailed. They were still a long way from the house. It had taken her a good hour and a half to make it to that valley in the first place. There's no way any horse could maintain that speed and still get her back home.

Holding the reins and rifle with one hand, Rachel patted her pockets. If only she could find her cell phone, she could call for help. Drat! She'd done it again! She'd forgotten it at the ranch! She shouldn't have gone into that shack alone, and she shouldn't have left the house without her cell phone. What a day to pick to be so stupid!

On one hand, she was on vacation from her job as an agent with Homeland Security. She had just finished working several cases with her boyfriend and partner, Dawson Tate, and her boss had promised her a few days of solitude to unwind. However, Rachel knew that solitude probably wasn't meant to include a break from her government-issued cell phone. She was required to carry that with her at all times, and yet she had an awful habit of forgetting the thing when she was working on the ranch. Home in Montana just seemed so far removed from what she did in New York as an agent that Rachel struggled with merging her two conflicting worlds.

Now her only option was to get to her cell phone at the ranch and call for help. She took deep breaths, trying to stay calm. She hadn't seen any other horses around the shack. The men there wouldn't be able to pursue her right away, which should give her a decent head start. But the ranch was still so far away! Yet she had no other choice. She would make it. She had to.

Even if she made it home, she wouldn't necessarily be safe. It wasn't as if she would find help as soon as she arrived. Dawson was out of town. Although he was her partner, he also still maintained supervisor duties in which she had no part in. While she got a break, Dawson had to fly to L.A. for some kind of meeting.

Her parents were gone for the day as well. Mom had gone with Dad to the appointment with his heart doctor. Rachel knew her mom had planned on coercing her dad into taking her shopping in Helena afterwards. They probably wouldn't be back until this evening. Their ranch hand, Xavier, wasn't scheduled to show up until feeding time.

So the house would be completely deserted, except for possibly her brother, Phillip. And he would be absolutely no help at all. Rachel fervently hoped Phillip wouldn't have arrived yet. She knew he was due for his routine visit sometime today, but she really didn't want him there to get in the way when she was trying to get immediate help in a volatile situation.

Every second ticked by as if in slow motion. She readjusted the leather reins in her sweat-slickened hands. All the muscles in her body were stiff and tense as she bent forward over the saddle, praying that Roosevelt would have the speed and endurance to get her to the ranch safely.

Oh, how she wished she had never even gone to that valley today! She hadn't been there for several years; why had she gone today? She tried to ride around the perimeter of the ranch's property at least once a year, but the land was so vast and rugged that it was longer than a single day's ride to do so. She usually had to camp out at least one night on those trips. The valley hiding the shack was a little inward of the far eastern property line, so she hadn't seen it on one of her more recent yearly circuits.

She wouldn't have been close to that area today if those stupid cows hadn't gone missing. She wouldn't normally be concerned about a few missing cows. They owned a lot of cattle and usually let them have free range in the summer. But they had been keeping a closer eye on this group because it included many of the new calves from this past spring. After a confirmed report of a wolf attack on another ranch in the area, they had stepped up their vigilance. When their ranch hand had noticed two cows and their calves missing for two days, Rachel knew she had to check it out.

But at some point, Rachel's ride had turned from work to pleasure. Truth be told, Rachel knew that there was no way those cows would have wandered so far from the others, but she'd been so thoroughly enjoying the ride that she couldn't resist a quick view of the beautiful valley that had been her favorite camping spot as a child. Then, after seeing that strange light at the top of the ridge, she'd been too curious to not check it out.

Now she would pay for both her indulgence and her curiosity. Images from the shack flashed through her mind. She tried not to think about them. She didn't want to allow her brain to analyze what she had seen. She knew whatever operation they were running was very bad, and she wanted to leave it at that. She was afraid that if she let her brain filter through the evidence and possibilities, she wouldn't be able to control the overwhelming panic that she was already fighting against. As it was, her emotions alternated between calm and outright fear, much as she alternated the horse between periods of full gallop and an agonizingly slow, restful trot.

Rachel tried to focus on creating a plan. Who would she call first? What exactly would she say? Top priority should be putting as much distance between her and that shack as possible. She would run into her room, grab her phone, and call on the way to her car. She would call Dawson first. He would know what to do. Then, if something happened, he could get the right authorities to her faster than anyone else.

The late summer sun beat down on Rachel and Roosevelt, filling the air with uncomfortable warmth and a bright eye-squinting glare. They were both covered in sweat by the time the buildings of the ranch finally came into view.

"Come on, Teddy," Rachel urged. "Just a little further." Her dad hated when she called his horse

'Teddy.' He insisted that since she had named every other animal on the property some girly name, he at least wanted a strong, masculine name for his favorite horse. But when Rachel was home, Roosevelt was all hers. In her mind, they had a special bond, and she was almost convinced that the horse actually liked it when she slipped up and called him 'Teddy.'

Rachel looked behind her. There was no sign of anyone following. She was too realistic to hope there would be no consequences for stumbling upon the shack. But maybe, just maybe, she'd have time to take off in her car and call for help.

Roosevelt was at a full gallop as she raced to the front of the house. Pulling him up sharply, she jumped off, leaving the faithful horse standing in the yard. She would make sure he got a good rub down later, but for now, she knew Roosevelt would like no greater reward than being left to his own devices around the ranch house. She was certain he would make full use of the water trough around the corner and the long green grass that was usually on the other side of the fence.

Hurriedly, Rachel leapt up the steps and across the porch, yanked open the door, and ran straight into someone.

"Hey, watch it!" her brother Phillip yelped, obviously annoyed at having the conversation on his cell phone interrupted.

Ignoring him completely, Rachel raced for her bedroom. Where had she put her phone? She frantically threw items off her dresser and blankets off her bed. Panic surged, her breathing coming in shaking gasps that were sounding more like sobs. Still no phone. Finally, yanking open her closet door, she rummaged around in the pocket of the jacket she had worn early this morning. Her fingers connected with hard plastic, and she pulled the phone out of her pocket.

Turning, she ran out her bedroom door as she pressed the buttons to dial Dawson.

Two rings. Almost to the front door. She heard the line pick up.

Rachel jumped in, not giving him time to even say hello. "Dawson, it's me. I'm in trouble—"

A hand clamped around Rachel's mouth from behind. Her cell phone dropped to the floor.

The hand was huge. It was a man's, and it pulled her back hard. While his left hand was around her mouth, his right snaked around, pinning her right arm. Rachel reached up with her own left hand and grabbed the hand around her face. But instead of trying to force it away, she pushed it toward her and opened her mouth. She bit. Hard.

She heard the man squealing. But still she kept biting as hard as she could. She tasted the dirt on his hand, and then she tasted the blood. The right arm pinning her went lax as the man suddenly wanted to get away from the pain she was inflicting.

The instant his hold eased, Rachel swung her right elbow back, hitting her assailant in a solid blow to the chest. Immediately spinning around, she landed a hard punch directly to the black-masked forehead. As he fell to the floor unconscious, Rachel finally released his injured hand.

Rachel felt something sharp hit her back, like a bee sting but worse. Quickly craning her neck and reaching back, she pulled something out and held it up. It was some kind of small dart. She'd been shot.

She spun, looking for the shooter.

There was no one. She had to get out of here. She tried to run for the front door, but her feet suddenly wouldn't move. They felt like they weighed a hundred pounds each. She forced them forward. Almost there. Fog swirled around the edges of her vision.

What was happening? She reached for the door handle. So very close. But she never felt the contact of the cold metal. Instead, she felt herself falling.

Then… there was nothing.

Chapter 3

Rachel gradually became aware of her own existence. She had the feeling that time had passed, maybe even a long time, but it was all blank like she hadn't even been alive.

What was the last thing she remembered? She searched through the blackness of her memory, straining until she caught a fragment. She remembered someone attacking her, but everything was very fuzzy. She thought she had gotten away. What had happened? She realized that, along with her groggy mind and stiff muscles, her back was sore, she felt slightly nauseous, and she had a fierce headache. Had she been shot with some kind of tranquilizer dart?

Rachel's senses slowly came alive. Where was she? She still wasn't convinced she wasn't in a coma. Everything was pitch black. Maybe this was just a more shallow phase where she could think.

She was lying on something hard. She reached out her hands, feeling all around. It was a rough wood floor. She slowly sat, running her hands along the floor until they connected with a wall. Carefully, she stood, putting her arms out both directions as she followed the solid walls along the rectangular shape around her. Was she in some kind of box?

Her right hand ran in to something cool and metal. A door knob!

She turned it. It was locked. She twisted it every way imaginable. She pushed and pulled, and then slammed her body into the door over and over. Nothing budged.

"Help!" she cried out, pounding on the door.

But the effort and sound made the headache and nausea worse. She felt as if she might pass out. Plus, since she wasn't sure where she was, she realized she may not even want her unknown captor to show up.

Giving up for the moment, she continued to slowly explore her cage. Several minutes later, her hands had gone over every inch of what she estimated was a six foot by four foot space. She still didn't know where she was, but she did know one thing. She was completely trapped. There was no way out.

Rachel sank back down to the floor, her back against a wall. She concentrated on deep breathing and tried to relax. At least she was convinced that she wasn't in some kind of coma, but her memories were still very fuzzy. She didn't have a clue where she was or how she got here.

As she sat, the tension slowly drained away, and she felt drowsiness creep along the edges of her mind. She couldn't see anything in the dark, but through the silence she heard the faint bubbling of a brook. Was she dreaming? She smelled the subtle aroma of pine and forest. It reminded her of starry nights spent camping. Nothing was more soothing than falling asleep to the lullaby of a gurgling creek and the aromatherapy of the forest. But the smell of pine didn't usually burn your nose. This had something sharp mixed with it, almost like a strong disinfectant. It was strange. She almost felt like she had encountered this same scent before.

Her eyes flew open in shock as she remembered.

Memories of finding the shack flitted through her mind. She recalled the awful realization that she had stumbled upon something dangerous and the terror of being shot at as she fled. Then she remembered racing to the ranch, finding her cell phone, dialing Dawson, being attacked... and then nothing. That's where her memories stopped.

But now, at least, she knew where she was and why she had been brought here. Someone had kidnapped her, taken her to the shack, and locked her in some kind of closet. But what did they want from her? Why hadn't they just killed her?

Rachel lay back down on the hard floor as a wave of hopelessness washed over her. No one knew where she was now or where she had gone earlier in the day. This shack was the perfect hideout. It was completely isolated, and she was the only one, other than her captors, to even know of its existence. Dawson and her dad would have no idea where to begin looking for her. These people couldn't keep her here indefinitely, and she was certain they would never be willing to let her go. Their priority would be keeping their secret safe. How long would they wait until they killed her?

The worries and questions filling her mind were overwhelming. Desperately, she began to pray. *Pease, God! Keep me safe. And get me out of here!* Not knowing what else to do or pray, Rachel simply repeated variations of the same simple prayer over and over, finally relaxing as the fog returned to claim her in sleep once again.

*****

A door slammed, startling Rachel awake. At the sound of voices, she sat up, seeing a faint sliver of light breaking the darkness at the bottom of the door. It must be morning.

"Lou, do you think she's still knocked out?" she heard a voice ask. It was a man's voice. He wasn't speaking very loudly, but his voice carried easily in the stillness.

"Probably," another male voice said with a slight snort of humor. "With the way she fights, if she was awake, we'd know. She'd be pounding the door down wanting to get out of there."

"What are we supposed to do with her?" she heard a third voice ask. This voice had a slight accent that sounded Middle Eastern.

"Nothing at the moment," responded the second voice, the one called Lou. "We're just supposed to keep her locked up. I don't know what he plans to do with her. I just know we're not supposed to kill her or do her any serious harm."

"Well, that will disappoint Mike," the first voice said. "He'll be itching to kill her when he gets back from the doctor. That wasn't a little nip she gave him."

At his words, Rachel suddenly remembered the details of being attacked. A man's hand had gone around her mouth and she had bit him to get away. It gave her a small amount of satisfaction to know that he'd had to seek medical attention for the injury. Her dad had taught her that nothing was off-limits in a fight for your life. She didn't feel bad at all for biting him.

With that memory came the rest of what had happened before she was knocked out. She knew now that she had been hit with some kind of dart in the back. She had tried to get away, but had fallen before she had made it to the front door.

"Frank, you'll have to talk to Mike," Lou said. "He'd better not try anything. You know how the boss is. If Mike does anything without his say-so…"

"He won't live long enough to feel happy about it," finished the voice with the accent.

"Speaking of which," Frank said, "we'd better get to work or we'll end up on the list too."

"Yeah," Lou agreed. "I'm sure the boss is going to want to move things up after everything that happened yesterday. He wants this project done."

With that, the three men fell silent for the most part. She heard them moving around the shack and occasional snippets of conversation, but they were obviously now focused on their work. She did learn enough from their conversation to figure out all three of their names and identify their voices. Along with Frank, there was Lou. And then Amir was the name of the third guy with the accent.

After a while, Rachel began making some noise like she had just woken up. She figured she might as well give them what they expected. That way, they would never realize that she had eavesdropped on their conversation.

Soon the man named Mike arrived. She heard them talking, but she didn't bother listening. She instead poured herself into the task of being loud and annoying. She didn't like just sitting there. Maybe she could anger them into doing something that would give her a chance to escape.

She yelled for help, pounded the door, kicked the door, and at one point even let out a long, high-pitched, ear-piercing scream that lasted a full ten seconds. But nothing seemed to work. For, although their threats escalated and grew more colorful, their actions did not. Finally, after the usually more quiet Amir let loose a particularly violently worded threat accompanied by something large hitting the closet door, Rachel consented to quiet down a bit.

"Are we sure she wasn't seen or didn't contact anyone else?" Frank asked.

"We're sure," Lou replied. "We arrived soon enough, and the brother was the only other one there. We entered the house before she had a chance to call or say anything. We took care of it. We also got her cell phone and location device on her watch. So put it out of your mind. We covered everything. It's time to stop yapping and do something useful."

Agreeing with Lou, Amir added, "One of you needs to go out back and check on our problem there. I have to monitor things in here. You know we can't ignore him forever."

"And one of you needs to take care of the problem in here," Lou said. "She's going to need some food and water."

What did they mean? Rachel thought in confusion. What 'problem' besides her did they have to check on out back?

Rachel's stomach dropped as sudden panic gripped her. *Phillip!*

Her brother had been at the house when she ran in. Lou said they had taken 'care of it,' but what did that mean? Had they captured him too? She and Phillip were about as different as a brother and sister could get. He was not at all equipped to take care of himself in a dangerous situation like this. While Rachel had thrived on learning ranching, weaponry and martial arts from their father who was ex-special forces with the Army, her older brother had held a strong aversion to such things and instead focused on gaining an education that enabled him to build a highly successful business.

Now the thought of Phillip being held captive choked her with fear and guilt. Though she and Phillip didn't see eye to eye on almost everything, she still loved him very much. She didn't know if she could handle it if she had somehow dragged her brother into a mess like this that got him hurt—or worse.

"Why don't you take care of her, Lou?" Mike retorted with an angry edge to his voice.

"I need to leave so I can make that meeting." Lou shot back. "After that, the boss wants me to take care of a bunch of other stuff. I won't be back here until tomorrow morning. You guys are on your own."

"I brought those supplies you wanted from town, Lou," Mike said. "I'll handle the problem out back and then bring those in from the truck. Frank can take care of *her.* "

"Mike, you can't do any of that with your hand done up like a Christmas present," Frank protested. "I'll handle things out back and with the truck, *you* stay and take care of her."

"Frank's right," Lou said, interrupting Mike's angry sputtering. "He'll go out back. You deal with things in here."

Rachel could hear Mike's grumbling as footsteps sounded across the floor.

"See you tomorrow," Lou called. "Don't forget your mask, Mike. You were wearing it at her ranch. She never saw your face, and we need to keep it that way. Oh, and remember. Don't kill her."

The door slammed shut, leaving Mike's unintelligible grumblings and angry stomping as the only sounds left in the room.

"What am I supposed to give her to eat?" he asked after a few moments of banging things around.

"Look around," Amir replied. "There's plenty of snack stuff lying around. Just pile a bunch of it on one of those big plates. Make sure you give her enough so we don't have to deal with her the rest of the day. Hand her a bottle of water with the plate and call it good."

After slamming things around for a few minutes, she heard footsteps coming closer to her closet door. Now was her chance. She had to get out of here and find out where Phillip was. There were only two guys in that room. She could handle that.

The footsteps came closer and stopped. Rachel waited. She heard a key in the lock. With a flash of humor, Rachel realized poor Mike was about to have a really bad day… again.

Chapter 4

Rachel heard the knob turn. Then a line of light appeared and got bigger as the door opened, stuck a little, then squealed open just enough for Mike to thrust a plate of food into the space. With his uninjured hand on the door knob, Rachel could see he had the plate balanced precariously on his heavily bandaged left hand.

The sudden light was blinding after so long in total darkness. Fighting through it, Rachel reached out as if to take the plate from him. But instead, she reached beyond, quickly grabbed his forearm, and pulled. Rachel swiftly planted a hard blow to his elbow, causing Mike to bend forward. She then reached around with her leg and kicked his calf. Completely off balance now, the large man fell forward into the closet. As he fell, Rachel landed one last blow to the back of his neck, right where it meets the hairline. She swiveled around out of the closet and firmly shut the door on the closet's new guest, confident that he was completely unconscious before his head hit the large, gooey jelly donut on the floor.

With her back to the closet, Rachel surveyed the room. A dark-haired man sat at a computer opposite her. At the sound of the Rachel's quick blows and the shutting of the closet door, he turned.

Amir.

Rachel's eyes collided with his. They were dark and flew wide open in shock. In an instant, Rachel took in dark middle-eastern skin, an angular face, bushy eyebrows, and thick dark hair. Though he appeared young, early thirties at the most, he had a hard look about him, and his eyes were devoid of any of the warmth or spark of the typical man his age. Instead, they appeared harsh and cruel.

Though their gazes locked for a fraction of a second, his image was forever seared into Rachel's brain. Amir bolted from his chair. Rachel saw the gun on the counter. Amir was taller and closer to the counter. She knew she couldn't beat him to the weapon. But she took off for it anyway, knowing she didn't have another option.

Amir's fingers connected with the gun, and he brought it up, aiming it directly at her chest. Detouring, Rachel grabbed an empty plate and two books from where they had been abandoned on a chair. Still in stride, Rachel threw the plate and books at him, one after the other. He dodged. The dish smashed into the wall. The book hit his shoulder and glanced off.

He brought the gun back level on Rachel. But she was too close now. With one spinning heel kick, she would be able to knock the gun out of his hand.

She planted her foot, but before she could pivot, she felt the impact to her back. Specifically, she felt three shots, each entering her back with a sickening thud.

She instinctively turned around, looking for who had shot her. But there was no one. Her vision dimmed, as if a dark, ever-thickening veil was slowly being drawn over her eyes. Was this what it felt like to die? Funny how there wasn't as much pain as she would have expected. She felt almost numb. She struggled with consciousness. A mere three seconds after the shots, all the strength emptied from her legs and she collapsed into nothingness.

*****

The first thing to penetrate Rachel's oblivion was the sound of groaning—the low, intense, guttural sound of someone in agony. Then she realized the groans were her own. She was the someone held captive by misery. Wave after wave of overwhelming nausea crashed over her. She wanted to melt into the floor. She prayed that the blessed nothingness would return, but instead, she only became more conscious of her suffering and the hopelessness of her situation.

She was back in the closet. Except this time, she couldn't move. Her feet were tied at the ankles, and her hands were tied behind her back. She found herself lying in a heap on the rough hardwood floor of the closet, unable to move and so miserable that every second felt like an hour.

She was going to vomit.

"Please help me!" she moaned softly. Then desperate, she gathered her strength, yelling weakly. "Help! Help! I'm going to throw up!"

She heard footsteps stop outside the door.

"Please," she begged. "I need a bucket and my feet untied. I don't think you want to clean up my vomit from the floor."

She heard voices, but her brain couldn't interpret what they were saying. Cold sweats raked her body. She kept swallowing, trying to keep her stomach from revolting.

The door opened. She closed her eyes, afraid the extra stimuli might make things worse. She heard the sound of something large being placed by her head. She felt the ropes around her ankles being stretched, and then they fell away as if they'd been severed.

She cautiously opened her eyes just a slit. A man was pulling away the rope from her feet while another man stood at the door with a gun pointed at Rachel. Both men wore black masks. Rachel realized they must have decided to not take any risks after her last escape attempt. It probably hadn't been the brightest idea to send Mike in alone last time. Now they didn't appear to be willing to make the same mistake again.

The men quickly left, shutting and locking the door behind them. Her muscles shaking, Rachel pushed herself up and drew the bucket to her. Her stomach heaved. She hadn't had anything to eat or drink in so long, she was surprised she had anything left to vomit up. Finally getting some relief from the remaining dry heaves, Rachel tried to grab the water bottle the men had left beside the bucket. Though they had left the cap off, there was no way she could bring it to her mouth to drink. Putting her teeth around the rim, she managed to tilt it slightly to one side and get a small amount of water to swish around her mouth. Exhausted, she lay back down on the floor and closed her eyes.

Finally, blessed sleep drew over her like a blanket. At one point, she thought she heard someone come back into the closet, but she couldn't rouse herself enough to make sure it hadn't been just a dream.

*****

Rachel startled awake. Unlike the time before, she knew immediately where she was and what had happened. She cautiously took inventory of her body, gently stretching each muscle. The nausea was gone for the most part, leaving her very weak and shaky. She remembered throwing up, but someone must have come and cleaned out the bucket while she was passed out. The smell Rachel remembered from before was gone, and the bucket now appeared empty.

She heard the front door open and slam shut.

"Amir! Where have you been?" She heard what sounded like Lou's voice.

"I had some errands I had to run," Amir replied.

"But you've been gone since yesterday when we got her back in the closet! Did the errands really have to take that long? We have a deadline to make!"

Amir didn't respond.

"What are you doing?" Lou asked, being met once again by Amir's silence. "Amir, WHAT ARE YOU DOING?"

"I'm going to kill her," he finally responded. Chills raced down Rachel's spine.

Chapter 5

"No, you can't," Lou said adamantly. "The boss hasn't given the order. If you kill her, your life is over."

"She saw my face!" Amir exploded. "My life is over anyway!"

"You don't know that," Frank inserted. "I'm sure the boss has some kind of plan for her."

"Do you have any idea who she is?" Amir asked angrily. "She's a government agent! I did some looking. She doesn't just own the ranch; she works for Homeland Security! There's no way we can let her live!"

Rachel heard Mike swear, then say, "That certainly explains a few things, like why she fights like a wildcat."

"Lou, did you know she worked for the government?" Frank asked suspiciously.

"Well, I… um… she didn't work for them a year ago."

"But you knew and didn't tell us? We just thought she was a Montana hick. Now we find out how dangerous she really is?" Frank's voice held barely restrained anger.

"Look, we all knew it was only a matter of time before she stumbled upon our little operation. We've all seen her riding around the ranch. We've even talked about how we didn't understand why the boss didn't just eliminate the problem."

"He should have let us get rid of her after the operation fell through a year ago," Mike grumbled

A year ago!

One life-changing event was burned into Rachel's mind from almost a year ago. But these people... this shack... couldn't be related to the attempted bombing in New York, could it? Dawson had assured her that she had just been randomly chosen to transport the bomb, that she had been convenient and not specifically targeted.

Rachel closed her eyes, remembering the words that had haunted her for the past five months. *"I should have killed you when I had the chance. You have no idea, do you? Life is just a crazy coincidence? That's fine. I have a feeling even mercy has a limit."*

John Riley's chilling words to Rachel had made no sense at the time. She had agonized over them and come up with no answers. But could it be that this was what he was talking about? Could there truly be no coincidences? Was it possible that she, Rachel Saunders, was the link in this seemingly unrelated mess?

"I don't know why he changed his mind," Lou was saying. Rachel tried to focus her whirlwind thoughts on his words. "He was willing to let her be the mule for our package, but then decided not to eliminate her after that was unsuccessful. Maybe he felt it was too risky to go after her a second time. He hasn't told me what his plan is, but I do know he has one. Just be a little patient, Amir. She isn't going anywhere, and we need to work on getting this project finished on time. She doesn't know what we're doing. We had the product finished and moved a while ago. Now we just need to finish the logistics and programming. Everything is in motion. She doesn't know enough to stop it. Trust me, we've planned too carefully; this one isn't going to fall through like New York."

And with the mention of New York, a fresh wave of nausea rushed over her, but this one had nothing to do with whatever she'd been drugged with. Her suspicions were right. Everything that happened then and was happening now was tied to two things: the attempted bombing in New York and Rachel herself. She was the connection.

"No. She needs to die now," Amir insisted. "I can't risk leaving her alive. She knows too much and she's already tried to escape once. It's not just me. I have to consider my family. I just got them into this country. I've managed to set them up with a nice life in New York under a different last name. My brother-in-law got a job at a factory, and my sister just signed a lease to open a Middle Eastern store and bakery. My niece, Tamara, just started first grade. Do you know how much work it has been to get them here and make arrangements to make it all seem legit? But they're here illegally! It doesn't matter that this girl knows nothing about the project. She knows enough about me. She saw my face. I know I'm in their database under a different name. It won't be so difficult to find me. If she can identify me, she can find my family. They'll be deported."

"You mean to tell me, Amir, that you want your family to live in the country you're helping to attack?" Frank asked incredulous.

"You have no idea what they've been through," Amir snapped. "Anything is preferable to that. And New York isn't the target this time. They're perfectly safe, much safer than back home. Besides, you are essentially waging war on your fellow countrymen. Doesn't that make you more of a hypocrite?"

Though obviously not American, Amir was the most well-spoken of the group. However, Rachel noticed the thickness of his accent increasing proportionally with his anger. It was becoming difficult to understand his words.

Rachel heard a scuffle as voices grunted and things suddenly crashed to the floor.

"That's enough!" Lou shouted. "Whether our loyalties or personal views fit in the mix is beside the point. We all share one reason for being here— money. If we are to see this project through and get the rest of that generous paycheck, we need to each stay focused and get the job done."

"I'll get to work on it right after I kill her," Amir said, determination in his voice.

"Amir, I can't let you do that," Lou replied quietly but with equal determination. "Just be a little patient. I'll talk to the boss and let him know what happened. She seems to be having a pretty strong reaction to those darts. There's a good chance she won't even remember seeing you."

No such luck, Rachel thought.

This time was different than the first time she had been hit with a dart. She may have had a more severe reaction to the sedative, but she also remembered every last detail before being hit. She could clearly recall every feature of Amir's face and every emotion of the last few moments before the three darts hit her back.

"We need to take care of this now!" Amir said adamantly, not accepting Lou's attempts to placate him. "It's too dangerous. Did you know that her boyfriend is also an agent? He's not going to easily give up on finding her. She may be incapacitated now, but what happens when she feels better? She almost got out the last time. You should have just let me shoot her with the gun, Lou. Then we wouldn't be having this problem."

"You would have never gotten a shot off, Amir. I saw how close she was to you. Another three seconds and you would have been as helpless as Mike. We're all very lucky that I came in at the right time and happened to be bringing in the dart gun the boss gave me."

"I'm not going to be using a dart gun this time," Amir retorted. "The sooner this is over, the better. I have to do this. Back up and let me take care of it, Lou."

Amir's voice was deadly quiet and calm now. Rachel's heart pounded.

"Let me be very clear, Amir," Lou said, his words sharp and cutting. "I will not let you kill her right now. Too much is at stake. I am not willing to put my life and everything we've worked for at risk so that you can kill her and feel better."

Silence. Rachel could feel the tension as she imagined Amir and Lou staring at each other, locked in a nonverbal standoff.

"I'll call the boss," Lou finally said, breaking the silence with his conciliatory tone. "He might just give the order to kill her after he hears what happened. But we have to do this the right way."

"Let *me* be very clear, Lou," Amir gritted back, not appeased in the least. "I don't work as long as she is alive!"

Amir's words were punctuated by the slamming of the front door.

Chapter 6

"Come on guys," Lou said wearily. "Let's give Amir a chance to cool off and get to work. "I'm scheduled to update the boss in a couple of hours. I'll talk to him about the girl then."

All conversation ended as the men apparently went about their separate tasks.

Rachel cautiously sat up from where she had been lying prostrate on the closet floor, too weak to move during the entire volatile conversation. She was finally starting to feel closer to normal. Though still weak, she could feel the strength returning to her muscles. Her hands were still tied behind her back. She began trying to work her hands into various contortions, trying anything to either loosen the rope around them or slip them free.

"Do you think we should go check on her?" Frank asked. "She's been asleep for an awfully long time."

"That's because Lou hit her with three darts!" Mike responded, somewhat gleefully. "It's a wonder that she's even alive!"

"Hey, the darts I shot her with were a lot lower dose than the one the boss got her with back at the ranch. He wouldn't give me the stronger darts because he said I would probably end up overdosing her. The weaker darts are nothing. I knew one dart wouldn't stop her.

"Don't get me wrong," Mike said. "I'm not criticizing. I would have unloaded a dozen on her if I could have. That would have taken care of Amir's problem right then!"

"You know," Frank inserted thoughtfully. "Maybe Amir is right. Maybe we should just kill her. If she can identify Amir, it wouldn't take much to connect him with us."

"I'm not opposed to killing her," Lou said. "I think there's too much at risk to leave her alive. But we can't kill her without the go ahead from the boss."

"Sometimes it's better to ask forgiveness than permission," Frank said quietly.

"I say we get it done now," Mike said firmly. "If we make the decision together, then the boss won't have much to say about it. He's not here to make the call, we are. It's not like he'll get rid of all of us. We're too close to being done with the project. He needs us too badly."

"We don't even have to tell him the truth," Frank agreed thoughtfully. "We could just say she tried to escape, and we had to shoot her since one dart wasn't strong enough to stop her."

Dread gripped Rachel. They were going to kill her!

They didn't know she'd been eavesdropping this whole time. They didn't know for sure that she remembered Amir and didn't realize half of what she'd figured out, yet they already considered her too dangerous to let live.

Her efforts to free her hands became frantic. She knew she was rubbing the skin raw, but she had to get out of here!

Lou was silent. Then finally, he responded. "Okay... we'll kill her. But, let me talk to the boss this afternoon and give him the chance to give the order. It'll be better for us if he does. If he doesn't, we'll still kill her, but claim that it happened when she was attempting to escape. Agreed?"

"I guess a couple more hours won't hurt," Frank offered.

"Just as long as she doesn't live past that," Mike said.

By their silence, Rachel realized they considered the conversation over and had returned to their work. They had acted as if she were of no more importance than the sack of garbage that needed to be taken outside before supper. They had decided that her life would end, apparently feeling no regret or remorse. Their only concern was to try to do it in a way so as not to get into trouble.

Well, she wasn't going to sit and wait for them to come kill her. If she was going to die, she'd rather do it fighting on her terms. They may kill her, but she was going to take at least some of them out with her.

All of her efforts with the rope around her hands had accomplished nothing. It was still just as tight, and her hands were just as useless as when she started, except now they were raw and painful.

Giving up on her hands, Rachel slowly rose to her feet. The dizziness was minimal; the weakness was subsiding. She wouldn't be able to use her hands, and her body wasn't going to be 100 percent. But she wasn't going to let that stop her. She could still probably inflict some damage. A simple plan formed in her mind. It probably wouldn't work, but it was the only thing she had.

She began stretching, concentrating on her leg muscles. It was already too hot and stuffy in the closet, and the day was only getting warmer. The longer she sat here, the more opportunity the stagnant, suffocating air had to sap what little strength she had left. After stretches and a few lunges, she sat back down, continuing to stretch the muscles that would aid in flexibility. If stretching was this awkward and strenuous with her hands tied behind her back, her more demanding plan was going to be nearly impossible to execute.

But she wasn't willing to wait. She still needed to find out where her brother was. He might be in worse shape than she was. They hadn't said anything more about him. Rachel's stomach flipped over at the thought that they may have already killed him as callously as they were planning to kill her.

She knew that, even though they said they would talk to the boss first, any one of them could change his mind at any moment and decide to end it now. Besides, she didn't know what the boss would say. He might want her moved or insist on something else that would make an escape attempt impossible.

There was one other reason she had to do this now: she really had to use the restroom. It had been late morning when she had been kidnapped. To her best estimates, that was at least twenty-four hours ago. She realized she must be extremely dehydrated, but it was a little ridiculous to think it had been more than a day since she had used a restroom. At this point, it was urgent, and she could not wait much longer.

Now was her best possible chance for escape. Amir was gone. She'd taken out five men in less than two minutes before, so three men shouldn't be a problem, right? She tried to ignore the shaking protest of her weakened muscles and the fact that her hands were hopelessly tied behind her and useless. She could do this. She had to.

"Please!" she called, trying to make her voice sound weak and miserable. "I really need to use the restroom!"

"Use the bucket!" Mike called roughly. "There's no way we're letting you out of there, so deal with it!"

"My hands are tied!" Rachel called weakly. "There's no way I can get my pants down to even use the bucket!

The men started arguing about what to do and who was going to do it.

"Please, help me!" Rachel called once more. "I'm going to be sick again!"

As the arguing grew more fierce, Rachel moaned and made retching sounds like she was vomiting.

Feeling around in the dark, she picked up the water bottle with her tied hands and carefully maneuvered to dump some of the water into the bucket. Standing, she then used her foot to soundlessly slide the bucket over near the door.

"I threw up!" Rachel called, her voice pathetic and filled with suffering. "Now the bucket stinks, and I still need to use the restroom!"

"Frank, it's your turn!" Mike said. "You'd better get in there!"

"It's not my turn!" he snapped back. "I'm not going in there. And I'm not cleaning up some girl's vomit!"

"Would you rather clean up her pee? Because she's going to pee all over herself and the closet if you don't get in there! And you'll be the one to take care of that too. I've already done my duty for the day. You haven't done anything yet!"

Frank was silent.

"Just get it done, Frank," Lou said, his calm voice contrasting with Mike's loud one.

"How am I supposed to let her pee?"

"Clean out the bucket first," Lou replied. "Then Mike can go back with you and hold the gun on her while you untie her hands. Retie her after she takes care of business."

"I don't like the idea of untying her at all," Mike muttered.

"Take your mask just to be safe, but don't worry about it. When we went in there earlier to clean up, she was too weak to even move off the floor. From the sound of things, it's going to be a while before she recovers. Get it done now so you won't have an even bigger mess later."

She heard Frank grumbling as he threw things around, apparently unhappy with the arrangement but unwilling to challenge both Lou and Mike on the issue.

Rachel stood, finishing her stretching with a few squats. Her back was wet from stretching in the warm room. Her empty stomach did gymnastics, and a sudden chill sent goosebumps over her skin despite the heat of the room. She tried to breathe evenly and calm her racing heart.

Dear God, I don't have the strength for this! Help me get out of here!"

She heard Frank's footsteps stomping across the floor. The key was in the door, turning the knob. As she got into position with her back against the rear closet wall, she had a sickening realization. There would be no dart guns this time. And Rachel knew that, within the next few moments, she may very well die.

Chapter 7

The door opened. Rachel reached out with her foot and kicked the bucket over, spilling water across the floor and onto Frank's pants and feet. Frank, obviously assuming the liquid was some kind of bodily fluid, let out a strangled, high-pitched shriek and began to tap dance in the water.

Rachel's right leg shot up in a crescent kick, interrupting his shriek and knocking him in the side of the head. He pitched forward, landing on his knees. Rachel immediately planted a front snap kick in the temple right in front of his ear. Frank dropped to the floor unconscious before the echoes of his shriek had cleared the shack.

Rachel jumped over Frank and the puddle of water, landing outside the closet. Two startled faces turned to look at her, but unfortunately, they were each on opposite sides of the room. She recognized Mike by his bandaged hand, but Lou was closer and already reaching for a gun.

He stood and brought up the gun as Rachel sprinted forward. She wasn't going to make it in time.

He fired.

At the last second, Rachel changed direction and dove behind a rolling chair. The bullet embedded itself harmlessly in the wall behind where Rachel had been.

Knowing the chair would provide little or no protection, she pushed it as hard as she could in Lou's direction. He easily dodged it, pointing the gun at her once again.

She had nowhere to go.

She watched his finger on the trigger and crouched, preparing to spring at him one last time, but knowing she'd never make it. A smirk of satisfaction crossed his face. He knew he had her.

Glass shattered. Lou fell. His finger never to pull the trigger; the smirk now permanent on his dead face.

Before Rachel's brain could fully register that Lou had just taken a bullet to the head, she instinctively spun to find Mike. He had turned back to face a computer screen, but now glanced over his shoulder at Rachel. Seeing her, he grabbed the gun beside him and whirled around, pointing the gun at her chest.

The door to the shack burst open. Without the pause of a heartbeat, a gunshot rang out. Mike dropped to the floor dead.

Dawson stood at the door, gun in hand.

"Is that all of them?" he called to Rachel.

Struggling to process the shock of what had just happened, Rachel nodded. Then she managed shakily, "There's one more, but he's unconscious in the closet. He'll probably be out for a while yet."

"Are you hurt?" Dawson asked, lowering his gun and walking toward her.

Still unsettled, Rachel's eyes went to Lou's body and then to Mike's. Her glance caught on the computer screen Mike had been looking at. Her breath caught in her throat. She ran over to it, desperate to change what she saw. Was this some kind of sadistic screen saver? She nudged the mouse with her knee. No.

"Dawson!" Rachel called, her voice strangled.

Her eyes locked on the screen, she felt Dawson come up beside her. She felt his body stiffen and knew she wasn't just imagining it. The computer screen displayed a timer, as in a stopwatch, and it was counting down.

"Get out! Get out!" Dawson yelled, pushing her toward the door.

Her body snapped into action. She ran even as her brain struggled to keep up. The last image from the computer screen was seared into her mind. The display had last read 8 seconds. Helpless to stop it, the countdown continued in her head.

8... 7... 6... through the door... 5... 4... 3... *We're still too close! We aren't going to make it...* 2... Whoosh! She was tackled from behind...

1... A massive, deafening explosion.

Rachel closed her eyes, praying, but unsure if she'd even used coherent thoughts. Smoke and debris filled the air above them. She felt Dawson's weight on top of her, covering and shielding her. Her throat felt on fire as the smoke burned like acid through her airway.

Would it never stop? She couldn't breathe! It was as if they were trapped in a doomsday disaster movie where the world ends.

Just when she feared that she would never breathe again, things seemed to settle. The smoke and dust lessened, and small particles were the only things left searching for a resting place.

She felt Dawson's weight shift off her back.

"Rachel, are you okay?" he asked, his own voice hoarse from the smoke.

When she didn't immediately respond, he pulled her into his lap as he sat on the ground.

"Come on, Montana, talk to me!" He cradled her close and smoothed her hair away from her face. "Tell me you're okay!"

Rachel blinked up at him and opened her mouth to speak. But before she could get any words out, a brutal bout of coughing wracked her body. Dawson held her as her frame heaved, helpless to do anything else. She was seeing dark spots in her vision before she finally felt she could breathe again.

Closing her eyes so the world would stop spinning, she finally whispered, "I'm fine." Her assessment of being 'fine' was rather ridiculous considering the coughing and dizziness, but it was apparently enough for Dawson as he ecstatically held her closer, trailing light kisses along her face and hairline.

Then her eyes flew open. "Let me go, Dawson! I have to go to the restroom. Bad."

Dawson, seemingly oblivious to anything she had said past the words, 'I'm fine,' continued cradling her tightly and murmuring, "Thank God! I've been so worried."

Rachel wiggled in his arms, struggling to get free. But her arms were still tied, and she couldn't seem to get Dawson to listen.

Instead, he was holding her like he'd never let her go and keeping a constant monologue. "I don't know what I'd do if…"

A strong, firm male voice interrupted Dawson's affections. "Dawson you have about two seconds until that girl of mine starts kicking you. I'd suggest you let her go."

Rachel smiled. She couldn't see him from this angle, but she would recognize her dad's voice anywhere.

At the sound of Carson Saunders' voice, Dawson must have suddenly realized what Rachel was saying. His hold immediately relaxed.

Rachel struggled to get leverage enough to stand with her hands tied. She felt her dad's strong, calloused hand grip her arm and pull her to her feet. Quickly, he used the knife he always carried to cut the rope binding her wrists.

"Phillip!" she cried, suddenly remembering her brother. "Where's Phillip? He was at the house when I was taken. The men made it sound like they were holding him out back somewhere."

She frantically began looking around for anything left standing that was large enough to hold a man.

"Hold on, Rachel!" Dawson replied. "Phillip is fine."

She looked at him, almost afraid to believe he was telling her the truth.

"He's at home," her dad provided. "He was never taken. We found him unconscious on the floor when we arrived."

Relief poured over Rachel. The men must have been referring to some other 'problem' out back.

"Is he okay?" she asked, practically dancing in her discomfort at this point. But she had to know.

"He's fine," her dad said. "He has a concussion and is concerned about you, but he's fine."

Rachel couldn't wait for any more details. She took off, looking for something that would provide privacy. Like an oasis in a hot desert, Rachel caught a glimpse of a tan-colored porta-potty that had previously been concealed behind the shack. So intent on her goal, she barely noticed that scattered rubble was all that was left of the shack. Thankfully, the sturdy toilet-in-a-box had apparently been far enough away to miss the full impact of the blast. She ran to it, feeling grateful to her kidnappers for the very first time. At least she wouldn't have to use the great outdoors.

Such relief! As she finished and doused her hands with the provided hand sanitizer, she heard what sounded like a helicopter.

Exiting the porta-potty, she shielded her eyes from the bright sun to see two helicopters closing in on their area. But the forest was so dense, it would be almost impossible to find a place to land.

Running back to join Dawson and her dad, she watched as the smaller of the two helicopters managed to land in the narrow clearing between the creek and what had been the shack.

"Reinforcements," she saw Dawson mouth as she shot him a questioning look. There was no chance of having an actual conversation with the noise of the two helicopters.

Instead of landing, the other one let down a long rope ladder. Five men in full combat gear were soon on the ground, and the helicopter quickly moved away. The first helicopter shut down, its rotor stilling as several other men disembarked. Rachel immediately recognized Andrews, her boss. After looking around at the destruction, he immediately walked over to the three of them.

"What happened?" he asked bluntly. Andrews usually had a much more pleasant manner, but from the grim expression on his face, Rachel knew he was not happy.

Dawson answered, "One of the men inside set off some kind of self-destruct sequence right before we took him out. Rachel and I barely made it out."

"And you couldn't have waited, Tate?" Andrews asked angrily. "I had a full team on the way. You knew that!"

"Do you think there would have been a different result?" Dawson snapped back. Dawson was the only one Rachel had ever known to talk to Andrews in such a way and get away with it. "Those helicopters weren't exactly subtle. It was probably less than ten seconds between the time Carson took out the first guy and the time I went in and got the second. He had obviously already been at the computer, ready to use that self-destruct as a weapon if Rachel came after him. Your team would have arrived on the ground right as the building exploded. Then you would have lost a lot more than any evidence inside. Besides, no, we couldn't have waited a second longer. Rachel's arms were tied and she had a gun to her head."

Andrews nodded, only slightly appeased. "It sounds like there was no way to prevent it then. We'll just have to see what evidence we can salvage." He turned to Rachel. "I'll get your full report later, Saunders, but right now, I need the cliff notes version of what happened and what you saw."

Rachel nodded and started to answer, but Andrews stopped her with a raised hand.

"I'm sorry. First of all, are you okay? Are you injured?"

"I'm fine, sir." Rachel replied, appreciating his concern. At his skeptical look, she gave her honest evaluation, knowing he expected nothing less from one of his agents. "I'm probably very dehydrated. I haven't had anything to eat or drink since being kidnapped. I'm still coughing, probably due to smoke inhalation from the explosion, same as Dawson. I was shot twice with a dart gun. The second time was a pretty hefty dose, and I had a bad reaction to it. But I'm doing better now."

Dawson looked alarmed. "Sir, obviously, we need to get her some medical attention. After such trauma to her body…"

"Yes, you'll need to take her back to the Saunders' ranch. I'll have one of our medical professionals take a look at her there. No hospitals or anything until we can be sure we have things secure and under control. But I am going to need that brief report before you go."

"Sure," Rachel responded. She hated when they talked about her like she wasn't there. If they would just be quiet for a minute, she could fill everyone in on what had happened. "Yesterday morning I rode out from the ranch, looking for some missing cattle. I stumbled across this place. It's our property; it shouldn't have even been here. When I realized this was some kind of bigger operation, I took off, but not before they saw me. They chased me back up the ridge, but I was able to make it back to the ranch. As I grabbed my phone and dialed Dawson, I was attacked. They had apparently followed me back to the ranch to ambush me there. They hit me with a dart gun, and I woke up back here at the shack.

"The men were using this shack to work on some kind of project," Rachel continued to explain. "I was able to eavesdrop on their conversation and figured out that they were part of the terrorist ring from the attempted bombing in New York! It wasn't random that they chose me to be the mule to deliver the bomb. They wanted me to die because they were concerned that I would discover their operation here!"

For some reason, Andrews and Dawson didn't seem shocked by her revelation at all. It was almost as if they had already figured it out. But, how? They had previously told her she had been targeted at random.

"Did you hear anything regarding future plans?" Andrews asked.

"They were planning another attack and were very close to executing it," Rachel replied. "But they never said what their target or date was. I just know it is supposed to be soon."

"Well, after this mess, it seems unlikely anyone left would be able to follow through on their plan, whatever it may have been," Andrews said.

"No, I'm afraid the plan is still in motion," Rachel said. "They talked about having already moved the project. It wasn't here. It sounded like they were making finishing touches on the preparations. Someone else was in charge. I got the impression that they were just pawns used to develop the physical device and the details of the attack. I don't think this will stop their boss from going through with it on schedule."

"Their boss?" Andrews asked, his tone urgent. "Who were they working for? Did you get a name?"

"No, I know nothing. They only referred to him as the boss. It seemed like the man called Lou was their primary connection to this man in charge. They never mentioned his name or gave any details that would give clues to his identity."

Rachel almost thought she heard Andrews swear under his breath. "So we have nothing. Our witnesses are dead. The evidence is destroyed. There's going to be a terrorist attack, but we have no idea where or when it will be. We have no idea who is behind it and have no clue to identify them.

"But you heard the names of the other guys, right Rachel?" Dawson provided. "And you at least saw the two faces of the guys we killed. If we can identify them, we might be able to link them to who their leader was. There were three of them who abducted you, right?

"There were four. But I..."

"Four? But there were only three in the shack. There were the two your dad and I killed, and you said there was another one you knocked unconscious in the closet."

"There was a fourth man who had already left. He's still alive. I don't know that you will be able to find any links between the other three and the boss. It sounded like the boss is very careful. Plus, the men didn't seem to be affiliated in any way. They were just employees interested in making money. But, if we were to identify the fourth man and capture him, he might be able to lead us to the boss."

At this point, Andrews seemed tired of the conversation and impatient to move on. "Okay, after you get back to the ranch, give Kelsey a call and start trying to identify the fourth man. She may be able to get a sketch artist by tomorrow morning. Then we could task our people with matching that up with someone in our database. It seems a long shot though. Even if we identify him, he'll be long gone as soon as he finds out what happened here. I've got to get to work on the scene here. Maybe we can salvage some clues. Right now, this seems to be our best hope."

Walking away, Andrews called over his shoulder. "I'll send Holmes over to figure a way to get you out of here."

"I think Andrews is wrong," Rachel said quietly, thoughtfully.

"What do you mean?" Dawson asked.

"The fourth man won't be long gone. He won't leave until he's killed me."

Chapter 8

"What do you mean, Rachel?" This time, her dad asked the question. Dawson was staring at her intently, as if trying to read her mind.

"I saw his face. I tried to escape one other time. Lou got me with three darts, but not before I saw Amir's face. He freaked out, thinking that I would be able to identify him and go after his family. He was determined to kill me, but the other men wouldn't let him until they had talked to the boss. It was a pretty tense argument. Amir finally left, saying he wouldn't finish his job until I was dead. He has too much at stake to let me live. He's going to come after me. I know it."

Rachel saw alarm and fear spark in Dawson's eyes before he was able to recover and mask his emotions.

Agent Holmes walked up, interrupting any response from the two men. Rachel had first met Holmes after the attempted bombing in New York.

Her impression at the time had been that he was a by-the-books sort of fellow and didn't care for Dawson at all. Though she had frequently encountered him since then when working in New York, she had found no evidence to change her original impression. She knew that Andrews was good at using his employees in ways to best suit their strengths. Holmes wasn't a field agent. In a lot of ways, he was Andrews' administrative assistant in New York and fulfilled whatever task Andrews needed done at the time. This was the first instance that she knew of, however, where Holmes had travelled away from New York with Andrews. Usually he stayed there to hold down the fort.

"Andrews said the three of you need to get back to the Saunders' ranch ASAP," Holmes said by way of introduction. "The problem is that we don't have a lot of options. We need this helicopter to remain here. The other one will be back to collect evidence and other agents in a couple hours. I can't alter that timetable for it to make a special trip and come back sooner. There is a road that was used by the terrorists, but it is rough and well-concealed from the main road. I could have someone come pick you up, but it would take a while for them to get here. Also, the road doesn't exit onto the main road anywhere near the ranch. It would take quite a while, probably 30 to 40 minutes just to get to the ranch from here. So, those are the options. There's not really a good way to get you out of here right now. Do you want me to get someone to come pick you up in a car or...?

"Never mind, Holmes," Dawson interrupted. "I guess we won't need your help after all. It sounds like we'd be better off to use the same transportation we used to get here—horses."

"Suit yourself, Tate," Holmes shrugged, turning and walking away

As Holmes had been talking, Rachel had been looking around at the rubble that was the shack. It was a miracle that she and Dawson had gotten out alive. The explosion had completely demolished everything and everyone left inside.

Rachel felt goosebumps as she realized just how much God had been protecting her. She had prayed that He would get her out, and He had. If Dawson and her dad hadn't arrived at just the right time, if her dad had been two seconds later firing that shot, she would be dead.

Speaking of which, how did her dad manage that shot? He had shot through the window, yet Rachel remembered that all the windows had been very high. She'd had to stand on her tiptoes to look in the first time she was here. There was no way her dad could shoot through, let alone get the right angle to make that shot. Unless… Rachel looked around. Her dad's horse, Roosevelt stood in the trees beside a beautiful new buckskin she had seen in the barn earlier.

As Holmes left in somewhat of a huff, Rachel turned to her dad. "Dad, did you get to use your show-off shot?"

The delighted grin of a little boy spread across his face. "You always thought it was ridiculous, but I told you it may come in handy some day."

"You did!" Rachel said, laughing.

"His show-off shot?" Dawson questioned, confused.

"He stood on the back of his horse in order to get the right angle to shoot through that high window, didn't he?" Rachel surmised.

At Dawson's amused nod, she continued. "He's spent countless hours training Roosevelt to stand still while he shoots. I always thought it was a waste of time."

"It was pretty incredible," Dawson said with a grin. "I wouldn't have believed he could shoot from standing on a horse, let alone make the shot, if I hadn't seen it myself."

"He didn't think I could make it," Carson said, still grinning.

"You had a lot riding on that shot," Dawson said.

"I know. It was my daughter's life. I wasn't going to miss."

"You needn't have worried, Dawson. Dad doesn't miss. You used your Winchester 45/70, right? I guess it doesn't really matter. Even when standing on the back of a horse, he doesn't miss, no matter what the weapon. Never let him make you wager on a shot, by the way. You'll always lose."

"That would have been good to know a couple months ago," Dawson grumbled. "Guess I should have known better since I've seen you shoot, Montana."

"Oh no, Dawson, you didn't! What do you owe him?

"A steak dinner!" Carson piped up. "And I'm still waiting for my payment, Dawson!"

Ignoring him, Dawson walked over to Roosevelt, preparing to mount. "We'd better get going. It'll be much faster to take the horses back than wait for Holmes to come up with something. We'd have to get the horses back somehow anyway. We'll need to ride double on Roosevelt though, Rachel."

Noticing Dawson's deliberate change of subject, Rachel sent an amused glance her father's direction and walked over to inspect the buckskin horse her dad would be riding.

"I saw this guy in the barn, Dad, but I haven't had the chance to ask you about him yet. He's beautiful," Rachel said, running her hands along the horse's light tan hide and black mane.

"Rachel, meet my new horse, Winchester. Roosevelt is yours now, Little Girl. I know how much you like him, and he seems to like you better than me anyway."

"Thank you Dad," Rachel responded, touched that he had just given her his favorite horse. "And what a beautiful horse you are, Winnie."

"Oh, no you don't, Rachel!" her dad said adamantly. His face was turning an amusing shade of pink. "His name is Winchester! You will not nickname my horse something girly. You can call Roosevelt whatever you want now. Teddy is fine. But you will NOT nickname my horse. His name is Winchester!"

With a serene smile her dad's direction, Rachel walked over to her horse and mounted behind Dawson.

Her dad on Winchester took the lead as they made their way back through the forest and up to the ridge. Rachel secured her arms around Dawson and leaned in to rest against his firm, muscled back.

She may have tried to seem normal and lighthearted for her dad and Dawson, but it was also an attempt to distract herself. The truth was, she was exhausted and scared. She closed her eyes, trying to block out the scenery swirling past, images that only reminded her of the terror of fleeing for her life only yesterday. She tried to comfort herself with the thought that God had protected her in so many ways already. He had protected her through racing up the sheer incline while bullets were flying around her, through being abducted, and through a destructive explosion.

Yet now, what scared her was a man—Amir. For some reason, he had always seemed to Rachel to be more dangerous, more deadly, than the others. He had been quiet, unemotional for the most part, until he had come back and argued with the others. He had been agitated, yet determined. She knew he would come after her. In his twisted mind, he would be doing it to protect his family, and he wouldn't rest until she was dead.

She had to do something. She wasn't willing to go into witness protection, and she wasn't going to sit around waiting for him to strike. She had to find a way to get out of this mess. And top priority was also stopping the terrorist attack. If only they could capture Amir, they might be able to do both things at once—eliminate the threat to her and get the information they needed to identify the boss and stop the terrorist attack.

Slowly, a bold, insane plan formed in her mind. She knew there was no way Dawson would go for it, but she'd just have to show him that this was their only option.

As they crested the ridge, Dawson pulled Roosevelt up alongside her dad, and they rode side by side. This ride home was taking much longer than her previous one, giving Rachel too much time to think.

"How did you find me?" Rachel asked her dad and Dawson, trying to strike up some sort of conversation. She couldn't talk to Dawson about her plan now anyway, and she needed to keep her mind occupied with something besides the trauma of what had happened and the worry over what would happen.

"It was actually your dad," Dawson replied. "When you called me, I heard you say you were in trouble. Then it sounded as if the phone was dropped and the line went dead. I panicked. I called Carson. He was already on his way back from Helena. I'm sure your mom had a wild ride. I think he made it home in record time, but by the time he got there, you were gone. Phillip was still unconscious. We had no idea what had happened or who took you. Your locator in your watch and cell phone were gone, probably destroyed. We looked up the history on your locators, but it was worthless since you apparently hadn't taken them with you on your ride."

Rachel, feeling guilty and ashamed, buried her face in the back of Dawson's shirt. She knew better than to forget her watch and cell phone. If she had just remembered to take them with her, then it was possible that none of this would have happened. They would have been able to locate her or at least track where she had gone on her ride previously.

"We had nothing to go on," Dawson said, refraining at this point from giving her the lecture she knew she deserved. "Phillip hadn't seen anything. He'd been hit in the back of the head and hadn't even seen it coming. He remembered you had come riding in on a horse, but he'd been on his phone and wasn't even sure which direction you'd come from. He actually thought it might have been the opposite direction from this one."

"I got a special government flight and arrived in the evening," Dawson continued. I'd already filled Andrews in, and he was making arrangements to come to Montana to head the search as well. But your dad and I weren't willing to wait."

Her dad took over the story. "I could tell Roosevelt had been ridden hard and long. Xavier said he thought you'd gone out this morning looking for those missing cows. The only thing I could figure was that you ran across something you shouldn't have. I thought the only way we were going to find you was to find what you had seen. Long story short, I tracked you."

Dawson jumped in. "We started out this morning after exhausting all potential leads and ideas at the ranch. It took a long time, but your dad was very impressive."

Carson continued, "Initially finding Roosevelt's tracks was the most time-consuming part, since it had been almost a full day at that point, and we didn't know which direction you had come from. But once I found them, it was relatively easy. You had been in a hurry. I knew you would have taken the most direct line possible to the ranch. It got more difficult again when we hit the more wooded area, but when we arrived in the valley, I had a bad feeling and went straight to our old camping spot."

"I called Andrews and let him know we had found a shack on your property," Dawson said. "We suspected this is what you had seen and thought you might be inside. By then, we were pretty sure we were dealing with terrorists."

"But how did you know?" Rachel asked, interrupting for the first time. "When I told you and Andrews that it was the same ring as plotted the bombing in New York, neither one of you seemed surprised. Yet you told me before that I was randomly chosen to be the mule."

Dawson answered with care, as if choosing words cautiously, trying not to upset her. "Let's just say we weren't surprised. There have been suspicions for a while that terrorists were using rural places in the Northwest, such as Montana, to headquarter their operations. We didn't know for sure, but we felt it was too much of a coincidence for you to go missing after having been a mule for a potential terrorist bomb. You haven't been working on any other volatile cases, so a terrorist connection was the only suspicion we could even come up with. Then, when your dad and I saw the shack squatting on your property, I knew for sure."

Too tired to know if she was fully satisfied with that explanation, she let Dawson continue.

"Anyway, Andrews instructed us to wait to enter the building until his team arrived. But your dad stood on Roosevelt and peered through the window using the scope on his rifle."

Carson reported, "I watched the man go to the closet and disappear; then I saw you come out. I saw another guy pull a weapon out and aim it at you. I knew I couldn't wait. Everything I saw, I told to Dawson, so right after I took out the one guy, he was ready and able to charge inside and take care of the other guy."

"It was so quick, so perfect," Dawson said. "I still don't understand how the guy at the computer could have set off the self-destruct sequence so quickly."

"They all seemed technologically savvy," Rachel explained. "I'm sure they had the whole thing set up to blow with just a few clicks. And Mike was more than a little paranoid about me anyway. I had beaten him up twice before. He probably had the sequence ready when he saw I had escaped. Then, when Lou fell, he simply activated it."

"When I saw that clock at less than ten seconds, I didn't think there was any way we'd make it out alive," Dawson confessed. "We almost didn't."

"We had no way of warning you about the bomb, Dad," Rachel said. "I'm so glad that you were far enough away to not be hit."

"I was still standing on Roosevelt so I could use my scope to see through the window," he said. "I was far enough away, but when I saw you two come tearing out the door and then hit the ground, I did the same."

As she thought about their narrow escape, she shivered involuntarily, despite the heat of the day. "Thank you, Dad. Thank you Dawson," she said soberly. "If you hadn't shown up right when you did…"

"God blessed us today," Carson said simply.

As they finally reached the ranch, Rachel's mom, Lydia, came running out of the house. Rachel's feet had barely touched the ground when she was practically smothered by her mom's embrace and drenched by her tears.

Before Rachel knew what was happening, her mom had her lying on a couch with a large glass of water, and a doctor was bending over her. Andrews had already made sure medical attention would be waiting at the ranch when they arrived.

After the doctor confirmed that she would be fine with lots of rest and water, Rachel showered and put on fresh clothes. Though she felt so much better after getting off all the grime from the past two days, Dawson and her parents immediately sent her to her room with strict orders to get some sleep. Rachel obediently went to her room and shut the door. But little did her well-meaning caregivers know, she had no intention of sleeping.

Chapter 9

Rachel turned on the power to the computer on her desk and used her phone to dial her friend and coworker, Kelsey Johnson.

"Rachel, I'm so glad you're safe," Kelsey said, immediately answering the line. "Andrews called and let me know what happened. Are you okay?"

"I'm fine for now, Kelsey. But, honestly, I don't think I'm out of danger. I need your help in finding some information."

"Andrews already called me in. I'm just getting ready to land in Helena, and the flight attendant is currently giving me dirty looks about being on my phone. If you can wait, I'll help you find what you need when I get there."

"I'm going to need the info sooner than that, Kelsey. I have a plan, and I need to have everything lined out before you even get here so we can get to work on it."

Kelsey paused. "Okay, Rachel. Tell me what you need. I'll text you passwords or instructions, whatever you need to access the databases. You already have a high enough clearance level, so it shouldn't be a problem."

Thanks to Kelsey's help, Rachel was soon able to find what she was looking for. It still amazed her that, with the right connections and access, almost any information on anyone could be located. Nowadays, secrets were difficult to keep with the government watching.

It had also helped that she had covered this type of research in her training last spring. While some of the weaponry and hand-to-hand combat classes had seemed unnecessary with her particular skills, she had gone through some other invaluable training for the job. Kelsey was the absolute best at this type of thing, but she herself had showed Rachel some of her tricks for locating even the tiniest needle in a haystack.

As she finished up, she sent several pictures and documents to her printer. Scooting her chair back, she stood to retrieve the papers, but stopped suddenly, hearing a commotion at her bedroom door.

"You are not going in there!" An angry voice said fiercely, though obviously trying to keep quiet. It sounded like Dawson.

"I AM going in there! If what you say is true, then we need to talk to her and get a plan right now!"

the other voice said forcefully. It sounded very familiar.

Rachel walked toward her door.

"She needs some rest," Dawson argued. "I'm not going to let you in there."

"I'm not asking your permission, Tate. Now move aside before I decide to reposition you myself."

Rachel smiled, now knowing exactly who was threatening Dawson.

"Garrett! You're here!" she called as she excitedly opened her bedroom door.

"Of course I am" Garrett responded, releasing his glare from Dawson to meet Rachel with a big hug. "There was no way I would stay away when I found out you were missing."

Garrett hadn't shown any romantic interest in Rachel since Miami, and for that, she was very relieved. Garrett had instead become a very good friend over the past five months. However, though he may have come to terms with her relationship with Dawson, he and Dawson still didn't seem overly fond of each other.

"How's Washington, DC?" Rachel asked, looking him over and trying to dispel some of the remaining tension between the men. Sometimes it seemed those two needed no excuse to come to blows.

Garrett made a face. "Hopefully, I'll be finished with this thing soon. It's not like we've made any headway. And this case is definitely not to my liking. I'll be glad to be done with it."

Though Rachel didn't know the details, she knew Garrett had been working a case in DC since they had finished their investigation in Miami.

Garrett continued, "But, right now, we need to talk about you. I'm sorry if I woke you, but when Dawson said…"

"Never mind, Garrett," Dawson said, his tone more than a little aggravated. "It certainly doesn't look like Sleeping Beauty was following orders anyway."

Rachel turned around and saw that Dawson was looking beyond the door into her bedroom and seeing that her fully-made bed was still unwrinkled and her computer was on.

"I need the story from you, Rachel," Garrett said seriously. "Dawson said you saw one of the terrorists' faces and that you think he's going to come after you. If that's the case, we need a plan. He's not going to wait long enough for you to identify him. He's going to hit quick."

"I know," Rachel agreed. "That's why I've been working on a plan."

Dawson ran a hand through his hair, his frustration evident. "Rachel, you're extremely dehydrated and recovering from dangerously high levels of a sedative. The doctor was adamant that you get some rest before you push yourself anymore. Your dad, Garrett, and I can take over your protection while you get some sleep. Andrews sent along some other agents for security as well. They're outside. You're safe for now. We'll work on a plan and have it ready when you wake in a couple of hours."

"Dawson, I know you're concerned," Rachel said, noting the lines of stress and worry lining her boyfriend's handsome face. "But this isn't something we can put aside for later. Garrett's right. Amir isn't going to wait. He'll make his move soon because he doesn't want me getting the resources I need to identify him. I already have a plan, but it's absolutely vital that I'm in on every detail. Besides, I don't think I could rest anyway, even if I wanted to. Don't worry. I'm fine. I'll rest after this is truly over and we catch him."

Dawson's gaze bore into hers. She didn't look away, but knew the instant he gave up. She figured he had probably learned by now when it was useless to argue with her.

"Okay," he said, resigned, but not liking it. "We'll do it your way. What's the plan?"

Unfortunately, Rachel knew he wouldn't be nearly so compliant after he learned what her plan actually involved.

Rachel peered around the two men and into the large front room. Her dad sat on the large, dark leather couch. Though he pretended to read a newspaper, Rachel knew he was listening to every word. Her mom was beyond him, nervously picking up items from a bookshelf and dusting beneath them.

"You said there was security outside?" Rachel asked.

"Yes," Garrett answered. "There are two men patrolling the area. Do you need them to come in?"

"No, leave them outside. Where is Phillip?" she called to her parents.

"He had a doctor's appointment in Helena," her mom answered. "He really didn't want to leave before we were sure you were safe, but he still has a nasty headache from his concussion yesterday. He probably shouldn't have even driven himself, but he insisted."

Rachel felt a shock of surprise as her mom turned to look at her. Her light blue eyes were swollen and red rimmed. Her normal blond, chin length haircut was uncharacteristically unkempt, and most surprising of all, Rachel wasn't even sure her mom had remembered to put on makeup this morning. Rachel had never known her mom to be awake for five minutes in the morning before having her full face tastefully and artistically applied. Lydia Saunders had always looked far younger than her years, but just now, her face looked haggard and at least ten years older than it did usually.

Rachel's gaze swung to her dad. He also looked terrible. When she had seen him earlier, she hadn't even had a chance to process his pale, weary features and the stress etching lines in the strong planes of his face. He had been looking the picture of health recently, even exceeding his cardiologist's expectations. But now, his appearance reminded her of the frail figure she had agonizingly prayed over after he'd had a heart attack nearly three years ago.

And she knew, without a doubt, what had caused the damage to her parents.

Crossing the room, Rachel swept her mother into her embrace, feeling her mom's shaking arms go around her and smelling the soft fresh scent of rosewater that clung to her hair. Her parents were both strong people, but she couldn't imagine the agony they had been through when she was missing.

For a few brief seconds, she let herself feel the terror of what had happened. What would have happened to her parents if she hadn't made it home safely?

Feeling another presence behind her, she turned into her dad's waiting arms.

"Come here, Little Girl," he said brokenly, smoothing her hair back and holding her close. With her mom, she had felt almost as if she was the one doing the comforting. Rachel was generally very successful at bottling up her emotions until she could deal with them. But, as she felt her dad's protective arms enfolding her, she felt her defenses begin to crumble the rest of the way. She took a deep breath, trying to stuff the trauma back down. She couldn't have a break-down now, there was too much she needed to do.

"As if sensing her need, her dad released her and stood back. "We need to get this guy so he can't come hurt you," he said with determination. "What do you need me to do?"

Instead of answering his question, Rachel turned to her mom. "Mom, I'm feeling hungry. Would you mind getting me something to eat while we discuss things?"

"Oh, sure, Sweetheart," she replied, her face brightening as if relieved to be given a task and doubly relieved that she didn't have to be in on the discussion. Rachel knew that, although her mom was very strong and capable, Rachel herself took more after her dad. Lydia Saunders was a peacemaker and avoided tense, stressful situations at all costs.

As her mom left, Rachel led the way back into her bedroom, motioning the men to follow her. At least she wouldn't have to worry about trying to keep Phillip out of the way. She definitely didn't need his kind of help underfoot. She shut the door and turned back to the three men. It was crowded in the room, but it was a relief to be sure they wouldn't be overheard.

"This room is clean," Rachel said. "I swept it for listening devices just yesterday."

Dawson grinned, clearly proud he had fully instilled some of his paranoid tendencies into her. She regularly swept her room and sometimes the entire house for any electronic eavesdropping. She may forget her cell phone and department-issued location devices, but at least her bedroom was bug-free.

"This conversation and this plan has to stay between the four of us," Rachel said. "No one else—not even Andrews."

"Rachel…" Dawson said, as if he suddenly didn't like the direction this was going at all. Funny how he was always fine if he was the one bending the rules, he just wasn't comfortable at all with Rachel doing it.

Rachel held up her hand to stop his objection. "Just let me explain everything before you try to talk me out of it."

Dawson obediently shut his mouth and folded his arms across his chest.

Rachel took a deep breath and launched in. "Amir will come after me tonight. He can't wait until tomorrow. By then, Andrews will have a sketch artist or whatever else we need for me to identify him. Putting me into witness protection until we locate him is not an option. If I disappear, he disappears. Also, we can't drag this out. There's some kind of bomb or other weapon out there set to be deployed in a terrorist attack sometime soon."

"Okay, Rachel, we get it," Garrett said impatiently. "So what's your solution?"

"The way I see it, we only have one option." Rachel paused, scanning the faces of the three men. She focused on Dawson. He had a sick look on his face, as if he knew what was coming. Rachel took a deep breath, speaking strongly and firmly.

"Use me as bait."

Chapter 10

Rachel waited for the explosions of protest, but none came. Instead, the men just stared at her, as if waiting for her to continue.

So she did. She outlined the simple plan to catch Amir and the role each of them would play. When she was finished, she watched the three men as they processed her plan in thoughtful silence.

Her dad was the only one making eye-contact. Rachel knew she could count on him. He trusted her and her abilities. Though he probably hated the thought of using his daughter as the bait in a trap, he would help in any way he could, knowing there wasn't an alternative to catching this guy. Besides, a lot of her basic strategy about luring your enemy onto your own turf, she had learned from her dad himself.

Confident of her dad's support, Rachel turned to study the two ridiculously handsome agents. They were both tall and dark, though Dawson's hair was black, whereas Garrett's was dark brown. Their strong masculine features were each enhanced by a pair of striking eyes, Dawson's blue, Garrett's gray. No wonder Rachel had fallen for each of them at one point. Each one was hard to resist, simply based on looks alone.

But the currently intense, brooding Dawson Tate was the one she loved, and she knew he was going to be the most difficult to convince. Garrett, on the other hand, wore a slightly amused expression, as if he was considering an outing on a warm spring day.

"So, just to be clear," Garrett finally said, breaking the silence. "Why aren't we filling Andrews in on this plan?"

"Probably because I've spent too much time with my paranoid partner," Rachel admitted, shooting a pointed look Dawson's direction. It was no secret that Dawson operated on the extreme end of trusting no one. "I trust Andrews, but he's going to want to have more people in on this. The more people know about our plan, the greater the chance of word getting out. These terrorists are obviously very well connected. We have no idea exactly how far their influence extends."

Dawson spoke up, "And, from the sound of it, there's no way Andrews would let you follow through on your plan for after we catch Amir."

Rachel grimaced. She had purposely skimmed over that part, knowing she would have an argument if she disclosed all of her intentions for that phase of the plan. But Dawson had apparently already heard enough to be suspicious.

"Why don't we just concentrate on catching Amir first; then we can deal with the next part," she said, hoping to sidebar any questions they might have.

"I'm fine with that," Garrett said.

After a pause, Dawson gave a brief nod of agreement.

"Dad?" Rachel asked.

"I'm in," he responded. "If that guy is coming for you, we might as well be ready for him."

"Good," Rachel breathed, relieved that all three of them were on board, at least for now. "The first thing we need to do is get Mom out of here. She needs to be safe and protected so she can't be hurt or used to get to me."

A knock sounded at the door. "It's Kelsey," a voice called.

Garrett opened the door with a smirk. "Miss Kelsey Johnson, may I say you have impeccable timing as always."

Kelsey sent a single scathing look Garrett's direction, and then turned a smooth countenance to Rachel. Well, it was readily apparent that Garrett and Kelsey weren't any more fond of each other than the last time Rachel had seen them. She knew they both had great respect for each other and their individual abilities, but they basically just didn't like each other—at all.

"Were you able to get the information you needed, Rachel?" Kelsey asked.

"Yes, thank you very much for your help, Kelsey. We were just going over the plan for tonight. "

Kelsey listened as Rachel briefly outlined what she had already gone over with the men.

"Are you okay with not telling Andrews about this until after we catch him?" Rachel asked hesitantly. Kelsey was usually a follow-the-rules kind of person; not to mention, she was often used as Andrews' right hand agent to get things done.

Kelsey nodded. "I understand the necessity, and I'm fine with it, as long as we fill him in immediately after we catch Amir. Don't worry, Rachel, you'll still have a window of time before

Andrews arrives. But he needs to know. As far as my involvement, I've been assigned to help you in whatever you need. So what is my role in all this?"

Worried Kelsey wouldn't like her task, Rachel explained in a rush, "I know you just got here, but I really need you to leave immediately with my mom and take her to my aunt's house. It's about three hours away from here. I'm afraid if she stays, she'll be hurt or used against me. Besides, there's no way Mom would want to stay around with something like this underfoot. Look, Kelsey, I know…"

"Rachel, I'll do it. Don't worry. I'm here to do whatever you need. I'll take your mom to your aunt's and make sure she stays safe until you give the all clear to come back."

"Thanks, Kelsey, I really appreciate it."

"What about your brother?" Kelsey asked. "Someone mentioned that he was staying here as well. Should he come with us as well?"

Rachel made a face. "That would be nice, but there's no way he'd agree. If I ask him to leave, he'll insist on staying. Our best tactic with Phillip is to keep him clueless. If he knows anything about our plan, he'll insist on helping and get in the way."

"We have enough security here to keep an eye on Phillip," Dawson offered. "He won't be nearly the target Rachel's mom might be. It's definitely more risky to let him know about the plan. He leaves in the morning anyway. We just have to tolerate him until then."

After that, things moved very quickly. Garrett left to run a few errands and ensure they had all the equipment they would need, Dawson worked on arranging the details inside the house, and Rachel's mom was soon packed and out the door. Rachel put on a brave front for her mom, hugging her cheerfully and pretending the fear in her gut didn't exist.

But as Rachel followed them out, she had mixed feelings. She was very grateful that Kelsey so willingly took the job of protecting her mom, but at the same time, Rachel felt sudden misgivings. She glanced at her beautiful, petite friend. With her long dark hair, porcelain complexion, and delicate features, Kelsey looked like she belonged more on a high-fashion photo shoot instead of a risky government operation.

In reality, Kelsey wasn't a field agent. She spent most of her time behind a desk. Even though this was supposed to be an assignment away from the action, there was great potential that Amir would realize the best way to get to Rachel would be through someone she loved. Would Kelsey be able to handle it if things turned dangerous?

After her mom was safely in the vehicle, Rachel turned to her friend.

"Kelsey, my mom is not at all like me. She's not a fighter. And you're not usually a field agent. If Amir decides to…"

"Don't worry, Rachel, I understand the danger. I may not normally be assigned as a field agent, but I am fully trained as such. Andrews often sends me on just this type of security mission. Remember when I guarded you after the bombing attempt in New York?"

Kelsey must have seen how distressed Rachel was feeling, for she uncharacteristically enfolded her in a gentle embrace. "You've got other things to think about, Rachel. Don't worry about your mom. Trust me. I've got this. I'll protect her as I would my own mother. No harm will come to her. I promise."

Rachel nodded, feeling the comfort of Kelsey's promise and trust in her friend wash over her. "Thank you, Kelsey," she said, too choked-up to speak above a whisper.

As Kelsey drove away with her mom, the screen door on the porch squeaked on its hinges as Dawson came outside to join Rachel. Coming up from behind, he wrapped his arms around her and pulled her back close to his chest.

"You shouldn't be out here," he said quietly. "It's too dangerous until we've caught Amir."

"I guess I didn't think about it," Rachel said, suddenly very nervous. Her eyes scanned the area around the house. "At least those security agents seem to be doing a good job of patrolling the area. Given the landscape and terrain, it would be difficult to get a good vantage point for a shot anyway. The area around the house doesn't provide much cover. Besides, Amir didn't strike me as an expert marksman."

"But still…" Dawson said. "You don't exactly strike anyone as an expert marksman either."

Rachel realized he was right, but as she turned to go back inside the safety of the house, she saw a car approaching down the long driveway. They waited on the porch as Phillip brought his luxury BMW to a stop.

He jumped from the car, ran up the steps, and crushed Rachel in a hug. She was so shocked she couldn't respond. For years, Phillip had acted as if he could barely tolerate her. She didn't remember him ever hugging her or being affectionate with her in any way, even as children.

"Rachel, I'm so glad you're okay!" he said, his voice choked up. "I was so worried!"

Rachel was touched. Maybe her older brother really did care for her after all.

But the next second, he released her and pierced her with a scathing look. "Do us all a favor, Rachel. Next time I'm around and you're in danger and running from bad guys, TELL ME! If I would have known when you first came in, I could have maybe done something to prevent you from being taken and me from getting a lump the size of Texas on my skull!"

Chapter 11

This was more the Phillip she was used to. Although now she realized that, at least his current bad attitude, was masking his fear for her and what had happened. Maybe he wasn't so bad after all.

Nevertheless, she wasn't going to take any of his blame and mud-slinging. "If I remember right, Phillip, you were on the phone when I arrived. As usual, you were pretty vicious about any possibility of interruption."

"For Pete's sake, Rachel! Life threatening situations are a little different! You should have grabbed my phone and thrown it! Anything to get my attention and let me know what was going on!"

Rachel looked up at him innocently. "So are you telling me that, in some instances, I have your permission to rip your cell phone away from you and dispose of it as I desire?"

Phillip grimaced, as if realizing he may have granted her more license than he intended. "Well,…

it seems very unlikely that something like that will happen again. Hey, was that Mom I saw driving away in some car as I was pulling up?"

Rachel tried to mask her smile at Phillip's sudden change of subject. She'd let him off the hook, but she might give him a hard time again if he decided to be too annoying later. For now, it was just nice to know that, deep down, her brother really did love and care about her.

"Yes," Rachel replied. "A friend of mine is helping out and taking her to Aunt Mary's house. It's going to be a few days before the investigation wraps up and things around here get back to normal. Mom was already seeming stressed by everything. Since there was nothing she could do to help, we all agreed that now would be a good time for her to go visit her sister."

Phillip didn't need to know the details of why Mom was leaving. Just because Rachel had a new appreciation for her brother didn't mean she was going to fill him in on any aspect of their plan. She didn't trust him to do what he was told. More than likely, he'd just screw everything up and end up getting himself or someone else hurt.

"That was probably a good idea to send her away," Phillip agreed.

Again, Rachel was surprised. Phillip made it a policy to never agree with her or her dad simply on principle.

But then he continued, "It drives me crazy to see her stressed out and flapping around here like a nervous bird."

And there you have it. He really wasn't concerned about their mother as much as he was concerned about being annoyed! Typical.

Their conversation over, Phillip walked into the house. Rachel followed with Dawson behind her. Dawson always managed to keep quiet and not get involved when she and Phillip were arguing. Wise man.

Rachel's dad was sitting in the living room, cleaning his guns. Phillip, completely ignoring him, walked across the room, heading toward his room.

"Hey, Phillip," Rachel called, suddenly remembering why he'd been gone in the first place. "How was your appointment?"

Phillip turned around. "They did a CT scan to make sure everything was fine. That's what took so long. They didn't do one yesterday when I went to the clinic here in town. Everything looked fine, the verdict being a moderate concussion. Said I'll probably have bad headaches for a few days, but I shouldn't need Mom to wake me up every few hours tonight."

Rachel really looked at him for the first time and felt a pang of guilt. He was pale and looked as if he didn't feel well. Phillip was a handsome man, though Rachel didn't think he looked much like her parents or her. He was a little shorter than Rachel, which she knew he had never appreciated. His hair was darker and his eyes were hazel to her blue. Phillip had never been athletic, but he wasn't overweight. His facial features were very angular and he had a rather prominent chin. Mom and Dad had always said he resembled Dad's bother, their uncle Leroy.

Overall, Phillip could present a rather striking, imposing figure, which Rachel was sure worked to his advantage in his business dealings. But at the moment, he looked and seemed more like a child who was cranky and didn't feel well. Still, she couldn't help feeling at least partially responsible.

"I'm glad you're okay," Rachel said. "And, for the record, I'm sorry you got knocked over the head because of me."

Without even responding, Phillip turned and walked to his room, never once glancing in his father's direction.

"Polite sort of fellow, isn't he?" Carson Saunders said as Phillip's door shut.

Rachel didn't even know what to say. She didn't understand her brother's relationship with their father. The only thing she knew was that the tension was almost unbearable any time the two men were in the same room.

Up until a little over a year ago, she had thought that they had a good relationship. Phillip had never shared his father's interests, but Dad had always been great at supporting Phillip in his own individual interests. Then something changed, and Rachel noticed a significant animosity between the two.

She herself had always had a hard time getting along with her brother, thinking him consistently selfish and disrespectful toward her parents, but she had always tried to hold her tongue. However, now it was even more difficult with this new tension.

Despite everything, Phillip still made regular visits to Montana to visit, even though he seemed to make them only out of some strange sense of duty. He actually seemed to hate every second he spent here or in the family's presence, yet he was very religious about visiting every month or so. This had been one such visit.

Not having the energy to waste thinking about Phillip any longer, Rachel suggested that they get something to eat. Instead of making something only for Rachel before she left, her mom had made a simple feast for everyone. Garrett soon returned and joined them in a dinner of sandwiches and a variety of tasty side dishes.

Rachel ate hungrily, but then gradually lost her appetite as she noticed the sky outside darkening toward night. She was nervous. She knew the arrival of night would also bring Amir. What if their plan didn't work?

After everyone had eaten and the dishes were cleaned up, Rachel had nothing to keep herself busy. All of the preparations had been made. Now was the waiting.

After reappearing to eat, Phillip had received a call from work and was now firmly entrenched in his room, ironing out some issue of great importance via his Bluetooth. Dad and Garrett had retired to the living room where they were watching some old John Wayne movie on TV. At loose ends and too restless to stand herself any longer, she had to get out.

As she pulled open the door to step out onto the porch, Dawson stopped her with a hand on her shoulder.

"Stop, Rachel, you aren't thinking! If you insist on going out there, let me go first."

She must be more tired than she thought. She hadn't even considered the danger, she just knew she needed to get out. She let Dawson pass.

"Wait here," he ordered.

Rachel watched as he went onto the porch and pulled all the screens down, enclosing the space. The shades came in handy during the summer. With them, you could enclose the porch, then actually sit and enjoy the evening without the fear of being carried off by a marauding band of mosquitoes.

After finishing his inspection and preparations, Dawson gently pulled Rachel out onto the porch. Keeping to the shadows close to the wall, he pulled her against him and wrapped his arms around her. They were silent for several moments as they watched the sun's grand finale as it gave one final burst of bright glory before slipping beneath the horizon.

Finally, Dawson spoke softly. "Rachel, I think we need to reconsider going through with this plan. It's too risky, and we need more backup."

"What do you mean? We have everything prepared. Besides, ready or not, Amir is coming for me tonight."

"Yes, but if we talk to Andrews, maybe we can get someone to pose as you. That way, Amir will still be lured into the trap, but you will be far away, not in any danger."

"Dawson what are you talking about? I don't have body doubles. I'm a Homeland Security agent. I am the body double!"

"But this is different. It's too personal. Too dangerous. Montana, please, I don't want you to do this."

Rachel's eyes searched Dawson's in the fading light. He was pale and his eyes were shadowed, pleading with her to understand. He almost appeared ill. With all of the life-threatening situations they'd been through together, she couldn't ever recall seeing him look so desperate, so nervous, so fearful.

Rachel reached up and touched his cool face, caressing his cheek gently with her thumb. "Dawson, what's wrong?" she asked gently. "This isn't my first mission and it definitely isn't my first time in a dangerous situation. In fact, I seem to have a knack for finding them. We're partners. Andrews would have never assigned us together if he thought you wouldn't be able to trust me as an equal and allow me to take risks. You've never doubted my abilities before. For Pete's sake, you let me throw a bomb out of a helicopter and jump aboard a terrorist's moving yacht! And those things were even before I was officially your partner! We've worked other cases before since then. So what's changed? What's different now?"

Dawson closed his eyes for a moment, taking a deep breath. Then he opened them again, his tortured gaze piercing Rachel. "In those other situations, I didn't have time to think. It was spur-of-the-moment—necessary. I didn't have much of a choice. Then everything was over before I had a chance to process how much danger you were actually in. Now, I know what's at risk because I've had plenty of time to think. And we have a choice."

"But we don't have a choice, Dawson! Ready or not, Amir is coming. Deep down, you know that this plan is what makes the most sense. We've been over this type of thing before. Right after I finished my training, we discussed different scenarios and we agreed that we would never let our emotions cloud our judgment. You made me promise that I would never let you be used as a hostage or weapon—even if it meant taking that shot that could put your life in jeopardy. You promised the same. You said letting our emotions interfere with our jobs would be the most dangerous risk. We had to trust each other as agents and partners."

"But this is different."

"I don't understand," Rachel argued, feeling aggravated with the whole conversation. "How is it diff…"

"It's real!" Dawson burst, obviously frustrated and emotional. Running his hand through his hair, he sighed and continued quietly. "When we talked about those things, we were discussing possibilities. I thought I wouldn't have a problem with putting your life on the line. But it was all in the realm of 'what if.' When you disappeared, the possibility of you dying suddenly became very real. I imagined horrible things happening to you. I couldn't handle it. I panicked. I knew that it was very likely that your kidnappers would kill you if they hadn't already done so.

"Montana, I can't lose you," he said, his voice strangled. "I love you too much. I don't want to wake up to my life without you in it. Now that you're safe, I can't knowingly risk your life again. Not when I could protect you."

"Dawson…" she whispered, not even knowing what to say. There was nothing she could do to make this better for him. Nothing had changed except his perspective. She was his same partner, still capable and highly trained. She could handle this. And she thought that, deep down, Dawson knew that this was still the best plan and that they must go through with it.

"I know, Rachel. I know," he said, as if she had spoken her thoughts aloud. "You're going to go through with it. You have to. Just please don't die on me."

Rachel smiled. "Don't worry, Hollywood, I'm not that easy to get rid of."

Dawson wrapped her in a close, almost crushing, embrace. He held her in silence for a long moment. Then she heard him whisper a prayer. "Father, keep her safe. And help me to trust her to you so I can do what has to be done."

As he finally loosened his hold, Rachel stood on her tiptoes and placed a light kiss on the tip of Dawson's nose. "I love you too, by the way—even if you are completely maddening at times."

Rachel's attempt to lighten the mood seemed to fall flat. Dawson didn't crack a smile. He instead gazed at her hungrily as if trying to memorize her face. He reached his hand up to cup her face, his rough fingers gently caressing her smooth cheek.

She wished she could make things better for him. But she knew there was really nothing she could do to take away the fear and worry. This was something he had to deal with on his own.

Dawson bent until his lips met hers in a gentle kiss. Rachel tried to convey to him as much love and comfort as she could. But her response seemed only to fuel his desperation, and his gentle kiss soon caught fire in a hungry passion. They were usually so careful about not letting their emotions and physical connection get carried away. But there were moments with Dawson that scared her with their intensity and left her weak in the knees. Oh, how she loved the man!

Dawson suddenly stopped, releasing Rachel so abruptly she had to catch herself from falling backward.

"We'd better get inside," Dawson said, his voice shaky and breathless.

Rachel's brain struggled to transition. Apparently, she hadn't been the only one unnerved by the depth of passion between them. She managed to nod.

With Dawson's hand at her back, she headed back to the front door. As she opened the screen door, reality struck. Her heart leapt and seemed to settle like a rock into the pit of her stomach. But this feeling had nothing to do with Dawson's kisses.

It was now fully dark. It was time to set their plan in motion. Despite her bravado and reassurances to Dawson, she was terrified of what the next few hours would bring. Amir was coming for her, and she wasn't nearly as confident as she had led Dawson to believe. She knew that before this night was over, Amir would be captured or she would be dead. She had done all she could to prepare. At this point, all she could do was wait for her enemy to strike and hope she survived.

Chapter 12

Rachel lay in bed completely motionless, yet she couldn't relax. Every muscle in her body was tense, and her eyes were as wide as if they were propped open with toothpicks. Though it was pitch black in the room, that didn't stop her from the endless circuit of scanning every possible shadow.

For the first time in her life, a man was spending the night in her room. Well, to be more accurate, it was two men. And she was waiting, pretending to sleep, until the third man arrived—the one determined to kill her.

Garrett was hidden in the closet. Dawson was in the shadows by the curtains. Her dad was outside somewhere, probably on the roof.

She touched her gun under the blanket, trying to reassure herself with its presence. How was she going to endure the waiting? Time was passing so slowly, she didn't know if her nerves could handle it if Amir took hours to show up. Worse yet, what if she was wrong and he didn't show up at all?

The room was completely silent, the darkness almost oppressive. Everything was so silent; it was almost unbelievable that two men could be so soundless and invisible. She thought she had too much adrenaline running through her veins for sleep to even be an option. But as the minutes ticked past with no change, the stress and fatigue caught up with her, and her body began to succumb to the dark silence. She never even realized the moment she lost consciousness. In her mind, she was still wide awake, watching, nervous.

Something woke her. It wasn't until she startled awake that she even realized she'd been asleep. Her heart pounded. She listened. Nothing. Her gaze bounced back and forth, frantically searching the darkness. What had awakened her?

She was not alone. Someone was here with her. Someone besides Dawson and Garret. The sense of another presence was what had sent her from sleep to immediate fight or flight mode.

Her breath caught. She gripped her gun. The plan had been to let Amir get inside the house. Her dad was watching outside to make sure he came alone. Once they had lured him inside, they would spring the trap, and he would have no chance to escape.

But he was here now! She was sure of it! Where were Dawson and Garrett? She could feel the presence coming closer. What should she do? Would he try to kill her before the two men realized what was happening?

Suddenly she heard a thud, and then a grunt like someone had just been punched in the gut. Not willing to wait any longer, Rachel pulled out her gun and reached her shaky hand to touch the bedside lamp beside her bed. Light flooded the room, revealing Dawson holding a struggling man dressed in black from head to toe. Garrett had obviously just disarmed the man of a gun complete with a high-end silencer. Now, with a weapon in each hand, he turned both on the intruder. Rachel also joined her gun in targeting her would-be attacker.

With the light on, Dawson and Garrett pulled off their night vision goggles. Seeing he was outgunned and outnumbered, the man stopped struggling. Dawson snapped a pair of handcuffs on him.

Rachel jumped out of bed and approached their prisoner. She unceremoniously pulled off the black hood he wore over his face.

The uncovered face that stared back at her wasn't the one she expected. It wasn't Amir. Startled, she stood there in silence, staring at a man she had never seen before.

"Come on, let's get him out in the living room," Garrett said. "Then we can figure out what to do with him."

As they pushed him out of her room, Rachel followed, trying to find the words to tell the men they had the wrong man.

"He was alone," her dad announced as he entered through the front door and turned on the living room lights.

"That's not Amir," Rachel finally managed, her voice tight and shaky.

Three pairs of eyes immediately swung to her in alarm.

"Are you sure, Rachel?" Dawson asked. "Maybe you didn't get as good a look at him at the cabin as you thought. This has to be him. He was going to kill you!"

Rachel paused and looked the man over carefully. Could she be wrong? No. This man looked Middle Eastern, like Amir, but Amir was taller. This man was stocky and had a much fuller face. He looked more like a thug, whereas Amir appeared to be an educated, intelligent man who carried himself with an air of disturbing superiority.

"I'm positive," Rachel replied. There was absolutely no doubt in her mind. "I've never seen this man before in my life. He isn't Amir."

Garrett groaned and closed his eyes. "He hired a hit!"

"We should have considered this," Dawson said, his disgust and frustration apparent.

"It doesn't matter," Rachel's dad said. "We'll just have to get as much information out of this guy as we can. He has to know something about who hired him. Then we'll go after Amir."

The room was suddenly filled with voices as the security men from outside bounded into the room, concerned about the lights and disturbance. Also Phillip, looking tired and angry at being wakened by the commotion, joined the group as well. They had never mentioned any part of the plan to either Phillip or the other security agents, and now they were stepping over each other with asking questions and demanding answers.

Numbed by everything that had happened, Rachel stood apart from the others, still staring at the captured attacker and willing him to be someone different. She felt sickened by their failure. They had really accomplished nothing. Amir was too smart to let this hit man know anything about him. They would get no information out of him. Instead, Amir was now free to try to kill her again whenever he wanted. Would she even be ready the next time?

The men were caught in a fierce discussion about what had happened. After Garrett's brief summary of capturing a man intending on harming Rachel, Phillip and one of the security agents continued loudly flinging around questions, angry that they hadn't been told about what had obviously been an expected danger. After all, Dawson, Garret, and Carson were fully dressed and had been clearly lying in wait.

Rachel felt something at her back.

"Is this your Aunt Mary's house?" a sickeningly familiar voice said pleasantly. At the same instant, she recognized the pressure at her back. It was the barrel of a gun.

Amir.

He thrust his cell phone in front of Rachel. She looked at the picture on the screen. Though it was night, her aunt's small house was still clearly recognizable. She glanced down at the time. The picture had been sent to his phone five minutes ago.

Not waiting for her response to his question, the voice in her ear continued. "I have men surrounding your aunt's house. They have orders to enter and kill everyone inside if I do not send them a text every two minutes. Come with me now, quietly. If you say or do anything, everyone in that house is dead."

Rachel swallowed. Her eyes swung around the room, silently begging someone to look at her and see what was happening. But everyone was too wrapped up in their argument to notice that one of the security guards had slipped away and was now standing beside Rachel. And he was not a security guard.

She had no choice. She had to go with him and do what he said. He had a gun to her back and her mother's life in his hand.

Amir grasped her arm with his hand and led her toward the front door of the house. Nobody was even noticing their exit! Help! Rachel wanted to scream, but before she could think of some unnoticeable way to get their attention, they were out the door and moving rapidly to a car parked in the shadows.

His plan was working perfectly. Rachel realized now that the other intruder had been a distraction for Amir's real plan. He had somehow disposed of one of the security guards and took his place. She knew that the security guards had planned to rotate at some point during the night, splitting the shift to remain fresh. Maybe Amir had made his move at that time. Then, when the commotion started, he had entered the house behind the other agent, keeping back until everyone else was fully distracted, and then ambushing Rachel. It had been a bold plan, and it had worked beautifully.

Rachel's heart slammed into her chest.

Don't get in the car! Her mind screamed. Her dad had drilled her over and over that you never get in the car with your enemy. If you did, you were as good as dead. But she didn't have a choice. She couldn't let him kill her mom.

She knew she had a good chance of getting out of Amir's hold and disarming him. She'd done that type of thing before. She could feel her body's ingrained training, urging her to fight. She might be able to save herself, but it would cost her mom's life.

Fight, Rachel, fight! It was almost as if she could hear dad's voice urging her. She knew he would say that, in this situation, Amir would probably kill her mom regardless of whether she cooperated or not. She even knew that her mom would never want her daughter to get in the car, even if it meant her own life.

Amir pushed her closer to the car.

Her mind knew all the facts. She knew what she should do, what she needed to do. But she couldn't make her body obey. An image of her mom being shot at point blank range filled her mind.

Rachel was afraid.

Chapter 13

God help me! Rachel prayed desperately.

"Get in," Amir demanded, using the barrel of the gun to prod her into opening the car door and getting inside.

Suddenly she remembered. Her mom wasn't alone.

Kelsey.

Kelsey's words echoed through her mind. *"Trust me. I've got this. I'll protect her as I would my own mother. No harm will come to her. I promise."*

Without pausing to reconsider, Rachel's body jumped into motion as if it had been lit with an electric shock. She immediately stepped forward with her left foot and swung completely around. The sudden, unexpected motion caused Amir to lose his grip on her arm. As she turned, she swung her right arm down and around in a circular motion, knocking the barrel of the gun upward and enabling her to simply grab the gun out of his shocked, loosened grip. Stepping forward suddenly, she brought the butt of the gun down into the middle of his forehead. He didn't go down or lose consciousness, but Rachel knew that it would make him dizzy and disoriented enough that he wouldn't put up much fight for at least a few moments.

Amir couldn't hide his shock. He hadn't had the chance to even realize what was happening before Rachel held his gun in her hands and was pointing it directly at him.

His surprise dissolved into intense anger.

"Call off your men," Rachel said, lifting his cell phone from the clip at his waist and handing it to him.

Amir sneered.

"Rachel, are you okay?" The screen door banged as Rachel's dad burst out of the house, his voice alarmed.

"I need you, Dad!" Rachel yelled back, never taking her eyes off Amir.

As her dad rushed to her side, she handed him the gun. "This is Amir," she explained in a rush. "Watch him. Make sure he doesn't move." As an afterthought, Rachel added. "Oh, and do what you need to do, Dad, but try not to kill him."

Stepping a few feet away, she fumbled frantically, trying to locate her cell phone. Finally pulling it out of her pocket, she pushed a couple buttons and waited for the line to connect. The phone rang four slow, perfectly-timed rings, and then it went straight to voicemail. She ended the call and immediately pressed the redial button. Something must be happening. Otherwise Kelsey would have answered. The only reason Kelsey wouldn't pick up the call would be if she was physically unable to do so.

Rachel listened once again to the steady ringing of the phone. Her heart was pounding and her mind jumped through horrific images of what might be happening on the other end of the line. Come on, Kelsey! Pick up!

On the fourth ring, the line was picked up.

"We're okay, Rachel."

At the sound of Kelsey's calm, though slightly breathless voice, the air in Rachel's lungs expelled all at once. Then, realizing Kelsey and her mom were still in danger, she fought to regain her breath.

"Kelsey, Amir has men outside the house! You have to… ."

"They're dead."

"W-What?" Rachel asked, not understanding what Kelsey had said.

"Amir's men were outside the house, but they're dead now. I shot them. That's why I didn't answer the phone the first time you called. I was a little busy."

"Kelsey, how did you… ?"

"Rachel, I told you I'd take care of your mom. I spotted three men watching the house a while ago, but they weren't making any move. They just seemed to be waiting. Then a few minutes ago, they started shooting at the house as they moved in on us. I picked off the two in front. The one in back made it to the doorway before I could get him. Your mom and aunt are a little shaken but fine. Did you get Amir?"

"Yes, we got him. He was trying to use my mom's safety as an insurance policy. But we got him right before I called you."

"Good. Have you told Andrews yet? I need to give him a call and get a cleanup crew here ASAP."

"Give me five minutes. We'll call him and tell him what happened with you as well. I'll make sure he sends some help your way. And Kelsey…" Rachel paused. She didn't know how Kelsey had managed to shoot and kill three gunmen intent on killing everyone in the house. All she knew was that she was profoundly grateful she had. "Thank you. You're going to have to fill me in on the details later. I want to know how you managed to take all three guys out if they were attacking simultaneously at night with guns blazing."

"There really isn't that much to tell. I got some marksmanship tips from the best."

Rachel remembered the few times she had gone to a shooting range with Kelsey. At the time, she hadn't understood why her friend had wanted her to coach her in shooting. Kelsey was a decent shot to start with, and she didn't seem to need to be at an expert level, especially since she wasn't a field agent. Rachel had humored her and helped her anyway, and now she was extremely glad she had assisted Kelsey in taking her skills to the next level.

"Could you also have Andrews send a few more agents for security?" Kelsey asked. "I'm going to take your mom and aunt to a hotel for the rest of the night. They don't need to be around for the cleanup. But I would like to have some extra security around just in case these three weren't the only ones Amir sent after them."

"Good idea. I'll take care of it."

As Rachel signed off with Kelsey, she heard a series of thumps, like the sound of flesh hitting flesh. Whirling around, she saw Amir slump to the ground.

"Uh, Sweetheart," her dad called. "I know you said you didn't want him dead, but is unconscious okay?"

Rachel tried to suppress her smile as she moved to rejoin him. "Sure, Dad. Unconscious is just fine."

Rachel looked up in time to see Dawson charging down the front steps with Garrett on his heels.

"Rachel, are you okay?" Dawson asked as he rushed to her side. "We just realized you and Carson were no longer in the house.

"I'm okay," Rachel replied. Gesturing to the man on the ground, she continued, "Dawson, Garrett, meet Amir. He snuck into the house by posing as one of the security agents. He had men surrounding Aunt Mary's house and threatened to kill her and mom if I didn't go with him. Dad came out looking for me right as I disarmed Amir. I talked to Kelsey. Everyone there is safe, but she needs Andrews to send a cleanup crew. She took out the three men Amir sent."

Rachel could see the questions in Dawson's eyes, but he merely nodded at her brief synopsis. "Let's get him in the house and secured. Garrett, go ahead and call Andrews. Break the news and get Kelsey some help."

"You'd better be the one to do that," Garrett said. "You're much better at smoothing Andrews' ruffled feathers than I am. I think he likes you more. If I talk to him, I'm likely to get us all fired."

"Fine," Dawson relented. "Help me get Amir into the house, and then I'll call."

At least he's more cooperative unconscious," Rachel said as the men lifted and carried Amir's limp form into the house, one at his arms, the other at his feet. "Just out of curiosity, Dad, what did Amir try to do?

Her dad shrugged as if there wasn't much to tell. But before he could mount a reply, Garrett jumped in with obvious delight. "We saw it as we came out of the house. It looked like Amir went for the gun and tried to throw a punch. Probably thought to catch the old guy by surprise. I don't think he even realized what had happened before Carson knocked him out with a single blow to the forehead." Garrett's grin was wide. "Rachel, I definitely see where you get it. Your dad is one bad dude. I wish I had that whole thing recorded!"

Rachel rather wished he had it recorded too. Her dad had taught her, but she didn't know that she had ever seen her dad use his skills in a real-life situation. She was jealous at having missed it this time.

The men put Amir on the couch. Though her dad said he'd be unconscious for a few more minutes, they handcuffed his hands behind his back for good measure. While Garrett stood watch over their prisoner, Dawson took out his phone and headed back to the porch to call Andrews.

As he passed Rachel, he briefly pulled her close. "Montana, why didn't you say something to us in the house or put up a fight with Amir sooner? You were almost to his car. He could have seriously hurt you or worse."

Rachel buried her head in Dawson's neck, instantly remembering the terror of those few moments. "He had my mom, Dawson," she said, feeling somewhat reluctant to admit her less-than-heroic actions. "I was afraid."

Placing a gentle kiss on the top of her head, Dawson released her and moved to make his call. She knew he still had questions about what had happened. Garrett probably did as well. But Rachel was grateful that both of them seemed to realize time was a factor right now and were willing to save the third degree for later. If they didn't time this perfectly, Andrews would arrive and it would be too late.

Two minutes later, Dawson was back inside and barking orders. The other security agent was already outside trying to discover what had happened to his counterpart since Amir had taken the missing agent's place.

"Phillip," Dawson called across the room. "I need you to go get the spare bedroom ready so we can use that room to hold Amir. Make sure the room is secure with nothing in there that can be used as a weapon."

Phillip actually rolled his eyes. "It's 2:00 in the morning! Come on, man! You're sending me to clean a room?"

"Look, Phillip," Dawson snapped back. "You were upset that we didn't fill you in on the plan sooner. Now is your chance to be useful. We need that room readied before our boss gets here. The rest of us have other things we have to do, including making sure this guy doesn't have any friends out there waiting to ambush us. So do you want to be a part of this or not?"

With a scathing glare shot in Dawson's direction, Phillip turned and padded down the hall to the guest room. Though his slippered feet prevented any actual stomping, he still made his displeasure known, muttering the entire way until he entered the guest room and slammed the door to do his assigned task. Rachel doubted whether a child could have done a better job of throwing a tantrum.

"We have 30 minutes," Dawson said the second Phillip's door was shut. Rachel knew Dawson had mainly wanted to get Phillip out of the way so they could carry out their plan.

"That's not much time," Garrett said.

Dawson nodded. "That's all we have. Andrews wasn't happy, but he's coming immediately from his hotel. Carson, why don't you head outside and be our lookout? Rachel and I will get in position. Amir is starting to stir. Give us about three minutes and then bring him in, Garrett."

Rachel grabbed the file she had prepared and entered her dad's office. Sitting down at his desk, she compulsively began rearranging the pictures and desk calendar placed on the surface. Her mouth felt dry and her palms sweaty. She was more than a little surprised that Dawson was letting her do this. She had expected an argument.

She took a deep breath.

You can do this! she coached herself.

The door opened. A surprisingly alert Amir was escorted into the room. At the look of hatred set like a mask on his face, Rachel's confidence dropped to the floor like a rock. Sheer panic gripped her.

Within the next twenty-five minutes, she would either have her answers or be fired from her job.

God, help me!

She was about to interrogate a terrorist.

Chapter 14

Garrett seated a handcuffed Amir in the chair across the desk from Rachel. Then he left, shutting the door firmly behind him. Amir stared at her with scorn burning in his eyes. Rachel forced herself to hold his stare. It was all she could do not to look away and cower. Even handcuffed, something about Amir completely terrified her.

She tried to comfort herself with the thought that she wasn't alone. Though Rachel had insisted it was vital that she be the one to interrogate Amir and that she do it alone, Dawson had insisted with equal vehemence that she not be alone. They had finally settled on a compromise: Dawson could hide in the room and be available should Rachel need him, as long as it appeared to Amir that he and Rachel were alone. Now Rachel was relieved that Dawson was hiding, listening in just a few feet away.

After a full, silent minute of staring at each other, Rachel decided on a different tactic. The staring contest was getting them nowhere. If this was going to work, she needed to play it cool, almost detached. Her goal wasn't so much interrogation as much as it was intimidation.

With a calm she didn't feel, Rachel reached into her file and pulled out a large picture. Wordlessly, she placed it in front of Amir.

The change was immediate. The thick tension in the room suddenly faltered with Amir's unmistakable shock.

After the silence of a few seconds, Rachel spoke quietly, "You have a beautiful family, Amir. The Al Farran family, or should I say the Farrans seem very happy here in the United States. You dropped the 'Al' when you brought them here, didn't you?" Amir visibly cringed at Rachel's use of his family's American name. He no longer looked volatile or dangerous; instead, he looked ill, his skin almost having a green cast to it.

Rachel continued, "You obviously care very deeply for them. You've put so much work into helping them. You didn't just smuggle them into this country; you provided new false paperwork which granted them new identities with nothing to tie them to the 'Al Farrans' of the past. Now they're so successful! Your sister's bakery looks fantastic! And Tamara is such a cutie! It would be such a shame to have all your work wasted, all their dreams shattered with them being deported back to your home country."

Rachel looked directly into Amir's eyes, making her unspoken threat very clear.

"What do you want?" Amir asked through gritted teeth.

"Information," Rachel answered. "I need to know who you work for. What is the terrorist plot that you've been working on? What is the target? I need to know everything, and I need to know it quickly."

"And in exchange, you will leave my family alone? What guarantee do I have that you and your coworkers won't have them deported as soon as I give you the information?"

"You have no guarantees, except my word."

It had been relatively easy to locate Amir's family, given the facts she had overheard while kidnapped. It had also helped that the family was already in the system. While their connection to Amir was still apparently unknown by the US government, they were already known to be illegal aliens. Up to this point, the government hadn't chosen to act on the information, and Rachel was in no way going to let Amir know of their true status. To gain his cooperation, it was necessary for him to think that she held all the cards. Even so, she couldn't bring herself to outright lie to the man. She had developed her plan and was fully prepared to keep her end of the deal if Amir accepted it.

"I am the only one who knows about the Farrans' connection to you," she explained. "I haven't shown this picture to anyone or shared any of this information, even with my coworkers. If you cooperate, I will burn this file. I can't guarantee your family's safety in the future, but you can be sure that no one will hear from me anything about their illegal status or their relationship to you."

Amir was quiet for a moment before speaking. "If I tell you anything, I'm a dead man."

Rachel shrugged. "The way I figure it, you're a dead man anyway. You were right at the shack. The minute I saw your face, your life was pretty much over. If you somehow manage to escape, your boss will have you killed. You are the only one left on your team, and you're too dangerous to leave alive. You're a terrorist. If Homeland Security has their way with you, you will be tried for your crimes and either spend the rest of your life in prison or be given the death penalty. Cooperation is the best option you have. You're already a dead man. Maybe you can somehow cut a deal with my superiors later. What's in question now is your family and whether you want me to hand this file over to my boss."

Part of her hated that she was being so heartless, but she was running out of time. This was their best chance of getting Amir to talk. She had a feeling that once he was officially interrogated, he would clam up and not say a word. Countless American lives may be at risk if she did not get the information on the planned attack. She remembered Dawson telling her previously that sometimes an agent has to do things that would otherwise be wrong in order to fulfill the duty of protecting his or her country and the people in it. Maybe now was one of those times.

"Your time is up, Amir," she said. "My boss is going to be here very soon. So what will it be?"

"Burn the file. I'll talk to you. But only to you."

Rachel nodded, her heart rate accelerating. "Who do you work for?"

"I don't know. I've never seen him. I don't know his name. I was contacted anonymously for this job. Lou has always been the go-between for the team and the boss."

"Lou is dead. Are you saying that he was the only one who knew who your boss was?"

Amir shrugged. "The boss is very careful. I'm not even sure Lou knew who he was."

"But I heard Lou say that the boss is the one who shot me with the dart gun. Lou was there. He said the boss wouldn't give him the stronger darts that he shot me with the first time. Lou had to have seen him."

"He did, but he certainly didn't give us any details. I think that was the first time they'd ever met."

"Explain what you mean," Rachel ordered. "How is that even possible?"

Amir sighed. "Frank and I were at the shack on the day you found it. When we couldn't catch you, we called Lou. He and Mike were running errands around town and had a much better chance than we did of intercepting you at the ranch before you gave away our location. Lou called the boss and informed him. When they entered the house, Lou was supposed to take out your brother while Mike grabbed you. I guess the boss showed up after you beat up Mike. Mike said he never saw him. By the time Mike woke up, he was gone, your brother was out cold, and Lou already had you unconscious and in his car."

"So you have nothing?" Rachel said flatly. "No information on your boss, or even the intended target of your terrorist plot? You were just a willing pawn?"

At Amir's silence, Rachel continued, tapping her pen on the file in front of her. "Excuse me if I don't buy it. You've got to give me more than that. You're smart, Amir, even overly cautious. You can't tell me that you didn't glean any information about the project or about who you were working for, even if everything was kept quiet."

"I didn't say I knew nothing," Amir clarified.

Rachel waited. They were running out of time. They couldn't afford to have Amir stall.

"You know the target," Rachel said, prodding him impatiently. "I know you do. I heard you say that your family was safe in New York because that was not the intended target this time."

"Washington, DC," Amir responded. "I don't know specifics. I just know the target is Washington, DC."

"That's not good enough. I need more information than that. 'Washington, DC' tells me nothing—not where, when, how, or why. You haven't even said what kind of weapon you were working on. Look, if you're not going to tell me absolutely everything you know in the next two minutes, then let's just quit playing this game. I'll hand over this file to my boss, and you can continue this discussion with the professional interrogators."

"Look," Amir said in a rush. "I was just one of many parts to this project. The boss was always good at making sure no person was too vital or had too much information. I was doing some complicated programming on the project, making sure it had foolproof security, remote detonation, things like that. I truly don't know the specifics about the target or on the identity of our boss."

At Rachel's skeptical look, Amir hurried on. "But you're right, I did manage to use my skills to procure a little more information than I was supposed to know. I set up a small receiver so I could listen in on Lou's cell phone conversations with the boss when Lou came to our base. I overheard that all of the details and programming of the project were supposed to be completed by this weekend. A direct hand-off of the work was supposed to take place Friday night at the Governor's Ball in Helena."

"But you're not done with the programming. You said at the shack that you weren't done. They won't be able to complete the project without your work, right?"

"I'm done," Amir said, a remnant of a proud, evil gleam glinting in his eyes. "I always back-up my work on a portable device. My computer at the shack was destroyed, but my work wasn't. I just transferred it to my laptop and finished it in the afternoon, after you escaped and the shack was destroyed. The boss contacted me and offered information on how to best ambush and kill you. In exchange, I had to hand off my completed work."

"Which you did?" Rachel asked, dread filling her already upset stomach.

"Of course. I didn't meet anybody; I just did it in a drop according to the instructions the boss gave me. The destruction of the shack won't set the plans back much, if at all. Everything was backed up at a different location. The way I understand it, my part is just one of the pieces coming together Friday night. At that point, the key players will be given all the necessary components to move forward immediately with the attack."

"Do you know if the boss himself is going to be at the handoff Friday?"

"I don't know," Amir answered. "But with as much trouble as he's been having with you and losing the rest of the team, I would guess that he will be there to oversee the exchange if not do it himself. He seems to be getting pretty desperate to make this work."

"Exact time and location?" Rachel demanded.

"It's supposed to take place in two parts. The transfer of the actual weapon is to be outside. I don't know for sure where, but the hope was that the streets of downtown Helena would be too busy to have the exchange be noticed. The transfer of the program and other specifics is to take place inside. Again, I don't know where. The details won't be known to any of the players until the last minute."

"Rachel, time's up," Garrett said, sticking his head into the room. "Andrews is coming up the drive. I need to get this guy out of here and into the other room we have prepared."

Frustrated, she nodded. She knew she wasn't going to get any further with Amir anyway. His boss was obviously smart and never let any of his employees know too much information. The only reason Amir knew as much as he did was because he was smart too, and sought out more information than he was actually given.

Garrett took Amir by the arm and escorted him from the room.

"Amir," Rachel called before they reached the door.

Both Amir and Garrett turned back to her.

"What is the weapon?" she asked, realizing her captive had never really said what he had helped design. Part of her dreaded knowing what they were up against.

"A bomb," Amir replied without hesitation, the evil, proud gleam back in his eye. "A highly sophisticated, massively destructive, virtually impossible to disarm… bomb. It will make the one they attempted to use in New York look like a toy."

Chapter 15

Rachel swallowed, holding Amir's gaze once again. For all his cooperation, Rachel knew he still desired for his part in the project to be successful and the terrorist plot to succeed.

"Now I've told you everything," Amir hissed, his hatred for her once again apparent. "The file?"

Without a word, Rachel picked up the file and walked over to the fireplace that covered one wall of the office. Setting the file inside, she lit it with a nearby lighter and watched the flame engulf the pictures and other information she had collected on Amir's family.

She may not have gotten all she had hoped for out of Amir, but she was fairly confident his information was accurate and he had told her what he knew. Even though the file no longer existed, Amir surely realized that she could easily reproduce the information should she discover that he had lied.

Maybe a professional interrogator would have gotten more. They may not have much to go on, but they had more than they did 30 minutes ago. They had a location and an approximate time for the transfer of the bomb and schematics for the terrorist plot. They just had to find a way to identify the players and intercept the transfer. It may be a needle in a haystack, but at least they had a haystack.

Rachel turned back and met Amir's eyes again right before Garrett hurried him from the room.

Dawson emerged from his hiding place crouched behind the leather sofa in the corner. Holding her briefly, he whispered, "Montana, you did fantastic."

Then he led her back into the living room as Andrews came through the front door. Rachel cringed the moment she saw him. Though it was the middle of the night, Andrews' tall form was fully dressed in a suit. The lights of the room reflected on his bald forehead, but most noticeable in his appearance, was the intense, blazing glare of his gray eyes. Andrews was usually so calm and hard to rattle. Now he resembled a volcano ready to explode. Rachel hadn't ever seen him so upset and angry.

"So my other agent tells me you three decided to do a covert ops without telling anyone. Without telling me."

Dawson started to answer, but Rachel jumped in first. This had been her plan. She wasn't going to let Dawson and Garrett take the blame for something that was entirely her fault.

"Yes, sir." Rachel replied. "Given the circumstances, I developed the plan and requested that Dawson and Garrett inform no one."

"We all agreed," Dawson inserted, obviously uncomfortable with Rachel shouldering all the blame.

Rachel had always been on very good terms with Andrews. From the beginning, he had seemed to hold a special fondness for her and her abilities. She just hoped that fondness would cut her a little slack now.

"I can understand wanting to keep things hush-hush," Andrews bit out. "But I'm your boss, and I thought I'd proven myself to you long ago. I cannot understand or overlook you not telling me. I should suspend all three of you immediately!"

He suddenly looked around and asked angrily, "Where is Matthews? I don't want to have to repeat myself. I know he was as much a part of this mess as the two of you."

Dawson replied, "He's securing the prisoner in the spare room and guarding him until we know your plans."

"Sloane, go relieve Matthews and send him out here," Andrews ordered. "Guard the room until I finish here. Nobody goes in, not even to give the prisoner water, understand?"

The agent named Sloane nodded and scurried to his post.

Rachel, taking advantage of the momentary lull in the lecture, jumped in. "Sir, I realize that we did not follow protocol, but in times past, you've overlooked an agent bending the rules if they got results. Before you give us some well-deserved consequence, please consider that we apprehended one of the terrorists alive and now have information about the planned attack that is still moving forward."

"Information?" Andrews questioned, his anger immediately stalling. "What information?"

Rachel masked a smile. She knew her boss well. While he may not like the fact that he was left out of the loop, his number one priority was results. As long as they didn't commit a crime, she was confident that his ferocious anger would eventually turn to forgiveness and even praise for a job well done.

Although Garrett joined Rachel and Dawson to face Andrews, all thoughts of a lecture and disciplinary action were apparently trumped by this more pressing issue.

Trying to fill him in on the major points as briefly as possible, Rachel replied, "The terrorist ring has developed a highly sophisticated, highly destructive bomb. The intended target is Washington, DC. The bomb programming and final schematics for the plan are scheduled to be exchanged this Friday night at the Governor's Ball in Helena. Although Amir didn't know the identity of the leader of the terrorist ring, he seemed to think the boss himself would be there on Friday to ensure the successful transfer. We have to intercept that exchange. It's our only chance."

"How did you obtain this information?" Andrews asked sternly. "I never thought the three of you the type to use illegal methods of questioning."

"No, of course not," Dawson replied, his tone showing his offense that Andrews was even doubting. "Rachel did a superb job of questioning Amir. Nothing illegal whatsoever. I was in the room and have the entire interview recorded."

Rachel looked at Dawson sharply. She hadn't realized he had recorded the interrogation. While she didn't like the idea, she knew Dawson had done it for her own protection. Dawson's word wouldn't be enough if their treatment of Amir was called into question. They would need hard evidence.

"Good. I'll be needing that recording."

Out of the corner of her eye, Rachel saw Phillip come into the living room from his bedroom and flop on the couch, his face a storm cloud of anger and impatience. Her guess was that, after completing his assigned task of readying the spare room, he had gone back to his own to try to get some sleep. With all the noise, especially with Andrews' voice raised at the level it had been, sleep for anyone in the house would have been virtually impossible. Rachel felt a pang of guilt. Phillip had mentioned earlier that he was going to be catching a morning flight out of Helena. She felt a little bit bad that he would probably be facing a very full day of work with little to no sleep. But, then again, everyone here was probably in the same situation. There would be a lot to take care of with no rest in sight.

Andrews must have also seen Phillip enter the room as well; he immediately closed his mouth and stopped speaking about the case. Rachel knew he was always extremely careful. He never discussed cases with anyone who wasn't directly involved. Where Phillip was concerned, Rachel would still rather have him know nothing. He would only offer his unsolicited opinion, get in the way, and generally create more problems.

"I'll see the prisoner now," Andrews said. "I've already called for his transport to a secure base for questioning. They should be arriving shortly."

Rachel followed Andrews down the hall to the spare room. She guessed that he would probably try to ask a few questions and get some additional, or at least reiterated, information out of Amir himself before he lost all chance of direct communication with their only source. Rachel doubted Amir would say a word, but she felt she should at least be there.

The agent who had replaced Garrett stood outside the door. Garrett handed Andrews the key to unlock the door. Garrett had apparently been unwilling to let this new agent stay inside the room with Amir or even give him charge over the room keys. Though they had their differences, both Garrett and Dawson had similar philosophies as agents: trust no one. Smart men.

Andrews stepped inside the room and immediately stopped, his body tense. Rachel, startled by the sudden halt, almost ran into him. Moving to his side, she saw Amir. He was seated on a chair in the center of the room facing the door. The window was to his back. His hands were still behind him in handcuffs, and his feet had also been tied for good measure.

His eyes were blank. He had a bullet hole in his forehead. He was dead.

Chapter 16

Rachel stood frozen, staring at Amir in shocked silence. She felt Dawson and Garrett fan out behind her with weapons drawn. They searched the closet and every nook and cranny of the room.

Andrews calmly got out his cell phone and made a call. "I need forensics here ASAP. I have a dead terrorist. I need a full team immediately to go over this place inch by inch."

"The window," Garrett said, pointing to the glass. A small hole was cut in the glass right above the bottom and the entire window had been shifted up, letting in the night's breeze. This had obviously been how the killer had gotten access to the room.

"Carson!" Garrett called urgently. "We need your help!"

Rachel's dad appeared at the door, his eyes immediately taking in the situation.

"Time frame?" he questioned.

"Maybe five minutes," Garrett responded. "Everything was secure when I left. The killer can't have been gone from here for more than five minutes."

"Let's go," Carson said. Garrett and Dawson moved to follow. She knew they were headed outside to try to locate, or at least track, the killer. Her dad was the best chance of tracking the killer on a dark Montana night.

"Matthews, stay." Andrews ordered, putting his phone back in its clip on his belt. "Tate, take the two other DHS agents to help with your search. We know it couldn't have been them. They were with us at the time of the murder."

Turning to a very impatient Garrett, Andrews explained. "You were the last to see him alive, Matthews. We need to go over a few things."

As the other two men left, Garrett exploded. "I wasn't the last one! Agent Sloane was with me. Amir was alive when we both left the room and locked the door."

"You're not under suspicion, Matthews," Andrews explained impatiently. "But we need to identify any and all clues. Is anything different from how you left it?"

Garrett pointed to the partially open window. "Obviously, the killer entered from the window. That's definitely different."

A strangled gasp interrupted Garrett's report. Phillip stood, wide-eyed, at the door. Rachel realized that the commotion from the room would have drawn anyone's curiosity like a magnet. Unfortunately, with his eyes locked on Amir's dead body, Phillip looked as if he might be sick.

"But I locked the window," Phillip practically squeaked, responding to what he'd heard Garrett say. "I know I did."

Agent Sloane moved to lead an obviously distressed Phillip away from the crime scene.

"Yeah, Phillip, you locked it," Garrett reassured. "I checked it right before I went to get Amir. I also put an additional lock on it.

Eyes wide with shock, Phillip consented to be led away from the crime scene as Garrett continued his report. "Rachel's bedroom window had been locked as well, but that didn't stop the intruder from entering her room earlier with very little effort. These locks are very simple to jimmy if you know how, so I added my own safety measures to the window. It should have been secure."

Andrews' eyes lit up. "That's right, we have another prisoner—the intruder you apprehended from earlier. Where is he? We need to make sure he is secure and interrogate him immediately."

"Sorry, Boss," Garrett said. "Don't get your hopes up. He's handcuffed in the basement. I'm sure he's fine. There's no reason to kill him. He knows nothing. He spilled his guts almost before I even asked a single question. He's a hit man who was anonymously hired. He's not involved with the terrorist ring and was only given specific instructions as related to killing Rachel tonight. I'm sure we could tie him to a lot of his actual crimes, but with the larger scope of this crime, he's clueless."

As Garrett spoke, Rachel finally succeeded in getting her muscles to cooperate. She walked around the room, intending to get a closer look at the window.

"Nevertheless," Andrews was saying. "We'll have to let the professionals see what they can get out of him. "Sloane, go check in the basement and guard the prisoner until his transportation unit arrives."

Andrews paused. "Careful not to touch or disturb anything, Saunders."

Giving Amir's body a wide berth, Rachel walked toward the window, her eyes, trying to scan every inch of the room for clues. Suddenly she stopped. Embedded in Amir's back was a dart, probably the same type that had been used on her.

"The killer hit him with a dart before executing him," Rachel said, pointing to the evidence. Andrews and Garrett immediately came around to see for themselves.

"That would make sense," Garrett said. "He shot him with the dart and knocked him out. Amir wouldn't have had a chance to call out a warning. The kill shot was delivered from the front directly to the forehead, execution style."

Rachel heard the men discussing the probable scenario, but she was really focused on the window. Upon closer inspection, she saw that special tools had been used to actually cut into the glass and then disable Garrett's lock and security measures. The window had then been slid up to allow the intruder access. The cool breeze floated in from the open window, sending goosebumps up Rachel's arms. Something wasn't right about the window, about the whole crime scene in general, but she couldn't put her finger on it.

Andrews' urgent order was soon fulfilled by a helicopter depositing a team of crime scene investigators at the ranch. As they took over, everyone else was quickly ushered from the room. With Andrews busy leading the investigation and

Garrett involved with handing off the other prisoner to the team tasked with his transportation, Rachel felt at loose ends. Dawson and her dad were still outside, combing the area for any clues to the killer's whereabouts.

The other security agent had returned, reporting that he'd found his missing counterpart back near one of the barns. Though he was still alive, he had a head injury from being knocked unconscious when Amir had apprehended him, tied him up, and taken his place to enter the house. An ambulance was even now loading him to be taken to the hospital.

Though everything was chaos around her, Rachel felt as if she were in a fog. She paced slowly, thoughtfully, down the hall, through the living room, to the front door, and back again. She kept thinking about that window. What was it that was bothering her so much?

*****

Rachel sipped the coffee, hoping the caffeine would cause her tired brain to start functioning. How she hated coffee!

At everyone's insistence, Rachel had consented to lie down while the crime scene investigation of

Amir's murder wrapped up. She didn't think she would actually sleep, but she had. And now she wished she hadn't. A mere two hours after going to her room, Dawson had woken her, saying that Andrews was ready to discuss a plan now that all the other agents and investigators had left.

Waking had been like trying to claw her way out of a deep pit. It would have been better if she hadn't slept at all, for now the adrenaline was gone and sheer exhaustion was all that remained.

To make matters worse, when she had finally managed to stagger out of her room, she found that Andrews had received an important phone call and retired to Carson's office to take it in private. Rachel had retreated to the kitchen, planting herself on one of her mom's old vinyl chairs and begging a cup of bitter brew to bring her back to the land of the living.

It was about 6:00 in the morning. She wasn't sure where Dawson and Garrett were. They had disappeared right after Andrews had received his call. Rachel's brain hadn't been functioning enough to even process if they had told her where they were headed. The sun was already streaking the eastern sky, though, so if she had to guess, she would say they were probably out helping her dad with feeding the animals.

Phillip walked into the kitchen and made a beeline for the coffee pot. As his ear was glued to his cell phone, he didn't even glance in Rachel's direction. Though he was fully dressed in a business suit and clearly preparing to catch his morning flight, Rachel quickly realized this wasn't a call associated with work. Phillip's voice was different, gentle, not cutting and authoritative. He spoke so softly that, even with straining her ears, Rachel could only catch about every other word he was saying.

"Alright… Call you later… Love you, too." Phillip hung up the phone.

Rachel watched Phillip's back in silence as he prepared his cup of coffee.

Phillip had always had girlfriends, lots of them, but Rachel had never heard him tell one that he loved her. This one sounded serious. Now that she thought of it, she remembered her mom mentioning a few weeks back that she thought Phillip might be getting serious about a girl. Though her brother was an extremely private person and had never brought girlfriends home to meet his family, Rachel knew that he talked to their mother far more than he did anyone else in the family.

Hmm, maybe if she played nice, Phillip would share a little information. Phillip's love life might at least provide a good distraction for a few moments.

"Hey, Phillip, what time is your flight?" she asked conversationally.

"8:30," he replied flatly, not bothering to turn around.

Rachel figured that meant he would have to leave here in about thirty minutes. Since he wasn't going to make this conversation easy, she was going to have to kick it up a notch if she wanted to get any information out of him.

"I'm really sorry about, well... everything," Rachel said. "I'm sorry you got a concussion. I'm sorry you didn't get any sleep last night. I wish you hadn't been caught in the middle of any of this."

Phillip finally turned around, looking at Rachel intently as he sipped his coffee. "It's not your fault, Rachel. It's not like you asked to be kidnapped or wanted some assassin to come after you. I should have just gone and booked a room in Helena for the night. I did get a couple of hours of sleep between about 3:30 and 5:30. Don't worry about it. I'll be fine."

Wow, was Phillip actually trying to be nice? Usually Phillip made no secret of his displeasure, seeming to almost enjoy punishing someone if he felt he or she inconvenienced him in any way. Rachel didn't quite know how to respond to this new, nicer Phillip. She watched wide-eyed as he sat down on a chair across the table from her.

"Rachel, I know we haven't ever been close, but I've been really worried about you, especially when you were kidnapped. Are you sure this job is worth it? Wouldn't you be happier here at the ranch? It's what you've always loved to do."

Phillip didn't know the details of the terrorist ring or anything. All he knew was that his sister had been abducted in connection with her job. Then some assassin broke in and tried to kill her. Then another guy tried to abduct her again. Now the latest installment was a murder in their own home.

Most days she enjoyed her job, but there were some times she asked herself the same questions Phillip was posing.

Before Rachel could gather her thoughts enough to come up with a good response, Phillip jumped back in, "I wish I didn't have to leave right now. I wish I could stay around until all the loose ends are tied up. What if someone came after you again? I wouldn't be able to forgive myself if something happened and I wasn't here to…"

"Get another concussion?" Rachel smiled, showing she was only teasing. This protective concern from Phillip was entirely new. Rachel had spent most of her life thinking that her older brother didn't love her at all. Now she felt a special warmth for him, realizing that he actually did care for her. Maybe, just maybe, this awful experience would draw them together.

"Rachel, I'm serious!" Phillip protested. "You could have been killed!"

"I'm safe now, Phillip. We caught the man who was after me. There's no one left."

Phillip scowled as if he was still not convinced. "I still don't feel right about leaving you here with this mess going on. I'll have to look at my calendar. I might be able to come back this weekend. Maybe Friday."

Alarms went off in Rachel's head. She really didn't want Phillip around to make things more difficult. It was actually a relief to her that he was leaving.

"I don't think that will be necessary, Phillip," she said. "The investigation will be wrapped up by then."

"Well, maybe I could just help Mom and Dad settle back in after all the drama. Who knows? You might have to make another run back to New York. Mom and Dad might need the help."

Rachel knew her parents needed Phillip's help like they needed the sun to stop shining, but she couldn't say that. She knew the surest way to get Phillip to come back was to ask him not to.

"Well, don't change your schedule or anything," she said, trying a different tactic. "We know you're really busy."

Phillip nodded. "I'll check with my assistant. I know there were a couple of different options for this weekend, but I don't remember what they were or if anything was extremely important."

"Maybe, whenever you do come back, you could bring your new girlfriend. I'm sure that would help Mom and Dad out a lot."

Phillip smirked, as if he knew exactly how Rachel was trying to manipulate the conversation.

At Phillip's amused silence, Rachel lost it.

"Okay, Phillip, spill it! I heard you talking to her on the phone. I want details. What's she like? What does she like to do? How did you two meet?"

Phillip laughed, a sound Rachel wasn't accustomed to hearing from him. Then, to her surprise, he actually began answering her questions.

"We met through work. She is very capable and independent, but very sweet. You would like her a lot. She's probably not my usual type of girl, which means you'll probably like her even more. Right now she's very busy with a project that should be wrapping up in the next few weeks. Maybe next month…"

Phillip stopped talking the second his dad entered the room. The sudden tension was a shocking and almost physical force.

"Good morning," Carson said, his warm greeting in no way masking the current between him and his son.

"Good morning, Dad," Rachel responded. "Did you get any sleep?

"A couple of hours, just like you."

Looking at his watch, Phillip stood and grabbed a muffin from the counter before heading to the door. "Gotta go. See you two later. Take care, Rachel. I'll call you for an update when I get a chance."

"Okay," Rachel said. "Have a safe flight."

The instant Phillip left the room, the tension dissipated like fog on a sunny morning, making it suddenly easier to breathe.

Rachel studied her dad as he rummaged through the refrigerator. Turning around with a loaf of bread in one hand and a peach in the other, he saw her looking at him.

"Have you heard any news yet about the investigation?" he asked.

"No. Andrews got a call right after I got up."

Carson walked over to the toaster, continuing to assemble his breakfast as he spoke. "We certainly didn't find anything outside. I couldn't track the killer. He left nothing to track, no clues, nothing. It's like he disappeared. I'll take a look again this morning, but we covered a wide radius last night. I think it's a dead end. We can't even figure out where he had his getaway vehicle."

Rachel didn't really want to talk about the investigation. She wanted to find out what was going on with her dad and Phillip. Maybe if she brought up the subject, her dad would open up. It had worked with Phillip; it was worth a shot.

"I had a good talk with Phillip just now," Rachel said, watching her dad's face carefully. "He was actually nice to me and worried about my safety."

Carson grunted, but didn't speak, continuing to butter his toast. But Rachel noticed the grim lines around his mouth at the mere mention of Phillip.

She continued, "I think he felt bad about leaving. It was almost as if he felt protective. He didn't want to leave if I was still in danger. I guess I didn't know he cared that much. He even said he might come back this weekend to check on everyone."

Still, her dad remained mute. Finishing his preparations, he brought his food to the table and sat down across from Rachel. He started eating as if Rachel hadn't spoken at all.

Rachel felt her frustration mount. Her dad was obviously not even going to mention the elephant in the room. He was just going to keep pretending that everything was fine between him and Phillip. But she hadn't imagined that tension.

She had tried to be patient and wait for one of them to tell her what was going on, but that was obviously not going to happen. Their relationship only seemed to be getting worse.

Rachel had had enough. She was stressed and irritable enough to take matters into her own hands. She was going to find out what was going on between Phillip and her dad, and she was going to find out now.

Chapter 17

"Dad, what's going on with you and Phillip?" Rachel wasted no time in asking.

Unable to avoid her direct question, Carson finally responded. "What do you mean? Everything's fine."

"Dad, I'm not stupid," Rachel said, exasperated. "Something hasn't been right between the two of you for a very long time. I've been waiting for you to say something about it, but you never have. Now it seems to be getting even worse. When he was here, the tension was so thick it was suffocating. And now I can't even mention him without an obvious rise in your blood pressure. What's going on?"

Carson sighed, "It's nothing new, Rachel. Honestly. You've been so wrapped up in everything that's happened over the past couple of years, you probably just haven't noticed it until lately."

"I have noticed it, but I thought it was just the usual drama with Phillip. He's never been easy to get along with, and his interests have always been very different from mine. But you and Mom always did a great job of encouraging him to be his own person. I thought, everything considered, that you had a great relationship."

"I thought we did too, but all that changed about the time of my heart attack. Phillip's personality has always reminded me of my brother. You know your uncle Leroy hasn't made the best decisions in his life. Your mom and I have tried to encourage Phillip in different, healthy directions, and for the most part, I think we have succeeded. I'm very proud of the success Phillip has become."

Rachel had always felt that Uncle Leroy was a very selfish person. He created drama where there was none and took advantage of those who loved him. She didn't know what he'd been like when he was younger, but she knew some of his bad choices had ostracized him from members of the family and even landed him in jail a few times.

"But..." Rachel said, encouraging him to continue. The silence stretched, but she waited patiently. She had the distinct impression that her dad would open up if she gave him enough time.

Sighing once again, Carson pushed his half-eaten toast away and looked directly at Rachel for the first time this morning. "I have no illusions about my son. His priorities are himself and his business, and I don't see that changing unless he turns his heart over to God."

Rachel had known that her brother's relationship with God had been a long-standing concern to her parents. Phillip had never shown a value for what he viewed as his parents' religion. She knew he pretty much lived for himself and even made disparaging comments whenever God or church was mentioned. She had seen an anguish for Phillip that her mother's eyes couldn't hide and heard both of her parents praying for him frequently. But that couldn't be the sole problem between her dad and Phillip. There had to be something else.

Now that he had started speaking, Carson's words flowed with increasing emphasis and emotion, as if the dam had finally burst. "He should have been more prepared when you were first attacked and kidnapped. If he hadn't been on that phone of his, he could have at least gotten some information from you and maybe even prevented your abduction. But nobody else is ever as important to him as himself. I'm glad you had a good talk, Little Girl, but don't get your hopes up about your brother. If he comes back this weekend, it won't be because he's concerned about you, or even your mother and me. It'll only be because he has to come for business. He never comes out of the goodness of his heart."

"What do you mean? He comes to visit about once a month, even when it seems like torture to him. I know it's hard to have him around, but I've always given him some credit for the effort, even if the only reason he does it is out of some strange sense of duty to you and Mom."

"Sweetheart, he doesn't come to see us. We are not the reason he visits Montana. He has business here. Real estate, I believe, though I've stopped asking what all Phillip does. This is where he started his business, and though he is now very wealthy and successful elsewhere, he still holds some property or business interests here."

Although Rachel was surprised, she quickly realized her dad was right. Phillip frequently took off during the day when he was visiting. She had just assumed he was looking for any excuse to get out of the house. She never really talked to him. This morning's conversation was probably the first time she'd talked to him, for longer than a 'pass the butter' pleasantry, in years.

"But, Dad, none of what you've told me so far explains what is going on now between you and

Phillip. There never used to be this tension between you. You mentioned something changed around the time of your heart attack? What happened?"

Carson paused. The look on his face scared Rachel, making her almost wish she had never asked; for in that pause, pain lined his face and made him appear at least ten years older than he was.

Nevertheless, he resolutely answered her question. "Immediately following my heart attack, even while I was still in the hospital, Phillip approached me about selling the ranch. I refused. He wouldn't let the issue drop, saying that I wouldn't be able to care for it anymore and that it would be best for the entire family if we sold. He was very persistent and very persuasive. I steadfastly refused and forbade him from even mentioning it to you. You were already so overwhelmed with managing everything else; I didn't want you pulled into our disagreement. Unfortunately, Phillip became very angry and nasty about it. I believe he was only interested in the potential money from the sale, which I didn't even understand. He has plenty of money as it is, but I guess he's always focused on more. He had great plans of even subdividing some of the land for houses in a type of luxury neighborhood. Absolutely ridiculous, in my opinion."

"But that was almost three years ago!" Rachel said. "Shouldn't you have settled your differences before now? You're right that I was probably too distracted with trying to take over the ranch and then with everything that happened involving Dawson and Homeland Security a year ago, but I have noticed the discomfort and sometimes outright animosity between you two. I think it's steadily been getting worse, not better!"

"Phillip won't let the issue drop. He keeps needling me and asking about it. He has let it make him very angry and bitter toward me, though he masks it very well around you and your mother. If we are ever alone together, it becomes clear very quickly that he feels almost a hatred toward me.

Rachel tried to think objectively. She knew how awful Phillip could act, and her natural tendency was to side with her dad completely and to be outraged at Phillip on his behalf, but that wouldn't help anyone. Instead, she tried to think about the issue from Phillip's perspective.

"Dad, you already know I would never agree to sell the ranch. I told you at the time of your heart attack that I loved this place and wanted to be the one to manage it. But honestly, Phillip should probably have some say-so in the decisions involving the ranch. It might make him feel more involved and responsible for it, which would be good since he'll inherit half of it one day."

"He won't inherit half."

"Of course he will," Rachel argued. "He's listed in the will as half inheritor. I'm the other inheritor."

"No, Rachel, it all goes to you."

Rachel was shocked. It was as if someone had told her the sky wasn't actually blue.

"Your mom and I made the decision long before my heart attack. We had everything drawn up legally to ensure that the entire ranch and all its assets be transferred to you upon my death. It's not even done as a will, so Phillip can't dispute it. The ranch is its own company with you being listed within it. Do you remember signing a bunch of papers about the ranch some years back?"

"I remember. But that was years ago, right after I turned 21! You said you were setting the ranch up as an LLC, but you didn't explain your reasons or the implications. I guess I assumed you had Phillip sign the same papers."

"I didn't want to make a big deal about it because I was hopeful that Phillip would mature some before we had to break the news to him. But that didn't happen. When he was so insistent on selling the place, I had to tell him, making it clear that he did not now, nor would he ever have any influence regarding the ranch. He was livid. It's not like I'm leaving him out completely. I have some other investments that will go solely to Phillip upon my death, but that wasn't good enough for him."

Rachel still couldn't overcome her shock to speak. Phillip was her older brother. She knew he had issues, but be was a good businessman. Why wouldn't her dad want him to have any of the ranch?

Seeming to read the confusion, her dad tried to explain. "We both know that Phillip doesn't care about the ranch, except as a dollar sign. He never has. You do. You understand that it's our family's legacy. I trust you to care for it. If the time comes that you have to sell or desire to do so, I don't have a problem with it. I trust your judgment and ability to make a wise decision. I don't trust Phillip's. I love my son, but there is no way I'm going to entrust any of the ranch to him."

Nothing her dad said about Phillip was a surprise to Rachel. She had long realized Phillip was a selfish man who wasn't interested in their family's ranch. What was shocking was that her dad was able to acknowledge his son's faults. And apparently, her mom had been in favor of this decision too.

She respected their choice, but it didn't fill her with joy to know the entire ranch would belong to her one day. Instead, she felt the weight of the responsibility and great faith her parents were showing in her.

Finally, Rachel responded, "I appreciate your faith in me, Dad. I love this place, and you know I will do my best to be a wise caretaker. But I can understand why Phillip wouldn't take that news well."

Carson nodded. "I tried to be very rational and explain that I knew he didn't have any interest in working the ranch. But it didn't matter. I don't know that I've ever seen him that angry. Things haven't been the same between us since then. Not that they were ever good before, but he's obviously still angry. He hasn't been able to forgive me and move on from the facts that I won't sell the property outright or at least leave it partially to him. I've tried to talk to him, especially for your mother's sake, but he is rude and only willing to discuss it if I'm willing to sell or give him what he considers his share. I'm not going to do either of those, so end of discussion."

Whether or not Carson meant the phrase to apply to this particular moment, their discussion was over the instant Andrews entered the room. Following on his heels were Dawson and Garrett, who immediately descended on the coffee and muffins like locusts happening upon a lush garden.

Andrews glanced at his watch and immediately launched into his report. "The investigation into Amir Hashim's murder has been wrapped up as much as possible. We're still waiting on a few results from the lab, but in all probability, we have no clues. It was as if a phantom entered the room, killed him, and disappeared. Our other prisoner has been safely transferred. Unfortunately, Matthews was correct. He seems to be a hired hitman who knows nothing of his employer or the motive for wanting Saunders dead."

"So..." Andrews continued, as if thinking aloud, "the only thing we really have to go on is what Saunders got from her questioning of Hashim."

Andrews paused, staring off into space as if deep in thought. The only sound in the room was of Dawson and Garrett rummaging through the freezer to look for more creamer for the coffee. Having tasted the bitter brew, Rachel knew they wouldn't be finding anything to improve it that much.

Finally, seeming to make up his mind, Andrews continued. "If your intel is correct, we'll need to begin immediate preparations for Friday. You three were right in that it's too risky to involve a large operation. Say nothing to anyone else about what you learned from Amir Hashim or what our plans are. We'll keep it close to the vest and work with a small team to intercept the bomb and other schematics. They can't know we're coming. I'll hand pick some agents to locate the bomb outside. We'll need to get some agents on the inside as well."

"I can get two agents into the Governor's Ball," Carson Saunders interjected. "I have two tickets. I get them every year, but Lydia and I have never bothered going. Political schmoozing isn't exactly my thing."

Carson Saunders probably owned more property than anyone else in the Helena area. With such recognition came a lot of respect and influence. He had been asked to run for local government numerous times, which he had steadfastly refused.

"Excellent," Andrews said in response to Carson. "I'll assign Tate and Saunders to use those tickets as guests on the inside. We'll probably get Matthews inside as well as a hotel employee. Kelsey Johnson will be outside assisting you. Mr. Saunders, you are under no obligation to assist us, but if you're willing, we'll position you with Agent Johnson as backup and to help identify people at the party. I'm assuming you'll know some of the players from this area."

"Count me in," Carson nodded.

It was interesting to Rachel that Andrews was even letting her dad be present in a top secret conversation, let alone asking him to be involved in the actual mission! Carson Saunders wasn't an agent. He had no clearance that she knew of. When Phillip had entered the room, Andrews had shut up like a vault. Rachel's only explanation was that Andrews had probably heavily researched her dad and his background in the Army's special forces. It was saying a lot of his high opinion of Carson Saunders if Andrews trusted him like that.

Rachel's focus returned to the plan Andrews was outlining. "You five will be assigned with apprehending the programming and schematics. I'll head up another small team to locate and intercept the bomb outside. We'll all have to be on the lookout for the person heading this operation. We have no kind of description, but I have a feeling he's someone with a decent amount of wealth and position. And we know he's dangerous."

Rachel listened as the four men continued to discuss the details of Friday night. Today was Wednesday. She knew there would be a lot of preparations with this being only the first of many discussions. But Rachel's mind focused on what Andrews had said about the man they were up against. Did they even have a hope of apprehending him?

They had managed to arrest one leader in this terrorist organization. But for all John Riley's wealth and position, he had been absolutely terrified to speak a word about his organization or his mystery partner. In fact, everyone who came into contact with this shadowy leader was inconsolable in their fear of him. Rachel knew that, in all probability, this meant he was more powerful, influential, and intelligent than anyone they had encountered thus far. With the exchange being made at a political event, there was a good chance that he was a political figure himself or at least had some serious connections.

And this dangerous villain had already tried to kill her at least twice.

As all these thoughts ran through Rachel's mind, she was left with an awful feeling of foreboding. They may be way over their heads on this mission. Most unsettling of all, however, was the realization that the over-riding emotion marking her sense of dread was pure fear.

Chapter 18

This is not working! Rachel thought with frustration as she smiled and shook yet another hand. Her dad's voice in her ear immediately identified the man in front of her as the Lieutenant Governor.

The Governor's Ball was in full swing. Rachel and Dawson had been mingling, purposely seeking out introductions with the other guests so Kelsey and Rachel's dad could identify those present and pinpoint any suspects.

So far, Rachel's flaming red evening gown had done the trick of attracting attention. Though she had garnered face time with significantly more guests than Dawson, they were still no closer to identifying one single suspect. And in Rachel's opinion, they weren't going to. The leader of the terrorist ring wasn't going to be sporting any red flags that would show up in their database right away. Otherwise, they would have already caught him. He was going to appear to be very legitimate and have the perfect background. They could spend the entire evening meeting every politician and wealthy guest in the room while the exchange took place under their very noses.

"We need a new plan," Rachel said under her breath as she turned to find Dawson. "We're getting nowhere with this."

"You're right, Rachel," Kelsey said. "Why don't you and Dawson take a spin around the room and just watch for anything that looks suspicious. At this point, your instincts are going to be more effective than identifying every face in Helena. Garrett is working the kitchen area, and Andrews is confident the outside of the building is completely covered. Maybe we'll get a break from one of those angles."

Having heard Kelsey from his own earpiece, Dawson met Rachel and swept her onto the dance floor.

The hotel's ballroom was noted as Helena's most luxurious setting. The light from golden chandeliers reflected off the glossy, marble-tiled floor. Women's dresses floated in a kaleidoscope of color around the room.

The setting and the Ball itself were designed to impress, yet Rachel instead felt almost offended by an opulence that seemed almost superficial. These were leaders who were supposed to be representing the people, protecting them and their interests in government, yet one of the ladies' designer dresses would probably pay for six months of food for a Montana family.

Rachel's family had always had their assets wrapped up in their land. While they had never been wealthy the way these people were, they had never been poor. But they did depend heavily on laws that protected ranch owners and their way of life. It was disappointing for her to see their leaders seemingly place such little value on their real jobs and the people who were depending on them. Seeing their attitudes made her realize that any one of them may be fully capable of leading a terrorist ring in targeting his own country.

Rachel felt her frustration mount. They had already sat through the political cheerleading and fund-raising speeches with no results. Now the alcohol, food, and dancing were flowing freely, and Rachel was beginning to worry that nothing would come of this mission. They had planned every detail so carefully, but maybe they had somehow missed the exchange of the bomb and schematics. Maybe it was even now on its way to fulfill its destructive purpose. Maybe the boss had discovered their plan and changed the meeting location. Maybe Amir had been wrong.

"Have I told you how absolutely beautiful you look tonight?" Dawson whispered in Rachel's ear. "You make it hard for a man to concentrate on surveillance."

Dawson must have felt her body tense as her mind raced and panic started to set in. She fully realized he was trying to distract her from her thoughts. He had already made his appreciation of her appearance very clear. When she had emerged from her room earlier this afternoon, he had managed to sneak her away and kiss her so soundly that she had to touch up her makeup and hair again before they left for Helena. Now, though he said she was making it hard to concentrate, Rachel saw that his eyes never stopped moving from scanning every square foot of the room.

Rachel smiled briefly at him, and then reported to Kelsey a couple that appeared to be in serious conversation in a corner of the room.

"Where did you learn to do this, Montana?" Dawson asked as they spun around the perimeter of the room. "If I had known you could dance so well, I would have taken you dancing long ago."

He was still trying to distract her. With a sudden ornery urge, Rachel decided to play along.

"Kelsey and I took a couple of dance lessons in New York when I was training and you were out of town. We thought it might come in handy. But honestly, I really learned from Garrett. We had to do this very thing when you were missing and we were looking for you. He's an excellent dancer, and it was all very… educational."

Rachel thoroughly enjoyed the look of jealousy that flickered over Dawson's face before he could mask it. Dancing with Garrett had been quite an experience, but there had been no romance between them since Miami. Rachel was very happy to feel that they had successfully developed a real friendship. While Dawson knew this, Rachel couldn't resist teasing him every once in a while. Adding to Rachel's delight, Dawson pulled her even closer, almost possessively, and now he legitimately seemed to be having difficulty concentrating.

"Montana, you're awful," he whispered, his lips tickling her ear. "Have you no idea what you do to me?"

Rachel looked up at him innocently, but she knew the amusement dancing in her eyes probably gave her away.

"We got it!" Kelsey shrieked suddenly. Rachel startled involuntarily, and her heart immediately began to pound. "Andrews' team just apprehended some men with what is believed to be a very sophisticated bomb. Our bomb squad expert is inspecting it right now to make sure it's the real thing."

Finally! The break we needed! Rachel's tense muscles turned to jelly at the rush of relief flowing over her.

"Keep on your toes," Kelsey instructed, calming slightly. "We still don't have the schematics or our villain. If that other exchange is going to take place, it'll be within the next few minutes. I'm sure they would have timed both events to take place around the same time, and once they figure out we're onto them, they'll disappear."

Rachel immediately began frantically scanning the room for anything remotely suspicious. It wasn't enough to get just a chunk of the terrorist ring and their plot. They had to end this now.

"Garrett just reported a suspicious male waiter heading for the ballroom," Kelsey reported urgently. He looks to be in his twenties and is short with longish, dark hair. The man showed up in the kitchen to work not too long ago. Garrett said he's acted nervous and hasn't done much of anything until he looked at his watch a moment ago and suddenly left the kitchen. He's headed your direction."

Rachel saw the man enter the ballroom. He was dressed in a waiter's uniform, but he wasn't carrying a tray or anything like the other employees roaming the room. He appeared to be in a hurry with a specific goal in mind.

Dawson turned, nodded to Rachel, and moved immediately on an intercept course. Rachel knew her job was to monitor the perimeter, taking in the big picture, while Dawson moved to possibly engage the target. It was Rachel's responsibility to identify any unfriendly accomplices, be ready if Dawson lost track of their suspect, and basically make sure her partner wasn't walking into a trap.

Rachel watched as the man weaved rapidly between the guests. No one was paying attention to him. Where was he going? He swerved and bumped guests in his haste.

Jerking around a large woman, he ran straight into a blond waitress with a full tray. Glasses and dishes crashed to the floor, drawing all eyes as nothing else could. The poor waitress's face turned bright red with embarrassment, and she bent to clean up the mess. The man bent beside her, quickly putting a few token pieces of glass on her tray before standing back up and moving rapidly away once again. Only one well-dressed lady bent to help the waitress as everyone else continued to gawk at her and the departing man.

Seeing Dawson following the man, Rachel followed at a distance, mainly concerned that she keep him in sight at all times. Rachel caught sight of Garrett, in the uniform of the hotel employees, also closing in on their suspect from the opposite direction.

By the time the man had reached the far side of the room, all eyes had abandoned him and the frivolity of the party had resumed. Slowing his pace, the waiter nervously looked both ways before approaching a man whose back was to Rachel. He passed very close to the other man's side, but never stopped. After smoothly passing, the man picked up his pace once again.

Rachel knew an exchange when she saw it. Their suspect had just slipped something into the other man's pocket.

"We have an exchange!" Rachel said to Kelsey. Dawson and Garrett had seen it as well, and they wasted no time in responding. Dawson intercepted the waiter while Garrett confronted the man with the suit. Seeing Dawson, the waiter immediately tried to escape, forcing Dawson to practically tackle him. Pinning him to the ground, Dawson bent his arms back and struggled to get a pair of handcuffs on him. The waiter fought violently to get away, all the while grunting and yelling loudly.

Once again, all eyes in the room turned to the dramatic scene.

At first glance, Garrett's encounter with the man in the suit was considerably less volatile. Garrett walked up and tapped him on the shoulder. Was this the man they had been looking for? Was this the powerful, elusive leader of the terrorist ring? Rachel saw Garrett say something. The man turned around fully, confusion and surprise written on his face. Rachel felt a bolt of shock run through her. The man was the Lieutenant Governor of Montana.

Chapter 19

Rachel fought the urge to go help Dawson and hear the conversation between Garrett and the Lieutenant Governor. Both men appeared to have things under control now, and she knew she was needed more as a sentinel.

"What's going on over there?"

"Hi, Phillip," Rachel acknowledged, continuing to scan the room and refusing to even look at her brother perched beside her elbow. "Dad said you had called to say you were going to be here tonight."

Rachel didn't mention that she had seen him repeatedly but had purposely avoided him. Finding out that Phillip was going to be at the Governor's Ball had just been another worry added to her already full plate. She hadn't wanted any chance of him finding out about their plans and seeking to get involved.

"I told you I thought I had something going on this weekend, but I couldn't remember what. My administrative assistant reminded me I'd received an invitation to this thing. I hadn't really intended to come, but since I'd wanted to come back here this weekend anyway, this gave me an excuse. I really dislike these things, but they're good for business."

Phillip certainly hadn't seemed to dislike the party tonight. Whenever Rachel had seen him, he'd been heartily schmoozing politicians and other wealthy peers.

More security and agents now joined Dawson and Garrett. Rachel guessed that, since they had successfully interrupted the exchanges, Andrews had called in reinforcements to assist. The guests in the room were transfixed by the drama before them. Some of them were closing in and making it difficult for Dawson as he tried to remove his prisoner from the room.

Phillip nodded toward the scene in front of them. "I take it this is part of your work and that it has something to do with the investigation. I figured you and Dawson probably weren't here just for pleasure."

Rachel didn't reply, but apparently, Phillip didn't currently feel the need for Rachel to keep up her end of the conversation.

"That's not surprising to me," he said, inclining his head to where Garrett was talking to the visibly upset Lieutenant Governor. Though he wasn't combative, the politician appeared to be highly offended. Garrett seemed to be having trouble convincing him to leave the room.

"And why is it not surprising?" Rachel asked, finally breaking her silence and taking his bait.

"I've always suspected he was dirty. In my experience, he'll promise one thing to someone, another thing to someone else, and then do neither one. He's seemed to have his own private interests dictating his public performance for quite some time. Of course, you could probably say the same thing for most of the people in this room. They're all pretty much snakes."

Maybe the Lieutenant Governor was the boss they had been looking for. Maybe this whole nightmare was about to be over.

"Okay, I'm signing off for now," Kelsey said through Rachel's earpiece. "Since we made our arrests, the operation here just changed and Andrews is already delegating a bunch of work my direction. Vehicles are already waiting to transport the suspects. I'm setting up headquarters with the state police. I'll see all of you there."

Garrett and Dawson were now moving the two men through the crowd to the exit. The Lieutenant Governor was now handcuffed, but still quite vocal in his protest.

Rachel should have felt relieved. It was over. They had caught the terrorist leader and now knew who had been behind everything. But she still felt an unsettled feeling in the pit of her stomach. After the terror of the past few days and the past year in general, this end had all been so easy. Maybe too easy.

Rachel knew she should follow Dawson and Garrett as they left. She would be expected to meet at the temporary headquarters too. But she couldn't get over the feeling that something was wrong. Her eyes scanned back and forth across the room, having no idea what she was even looking for. Everyone stood transfixed by the drama. The only person in the room not watching was the poor waitress who was still trying to clean up the mess off the floor. Finally standing, she lifted her tray of trash and broken glass and moved rapidly in the opposite direction. Her face was still beet red, and she looked as if she couldn't wait to leave the room and burst into tears.

There was something familiar about the waitress's face. She was blond, very pretty, and looked to be about Rachel's age. Maybe they graduated high school together. Rachel tended to be rather inept at remembering names.

"I've got to run," Phillip said, glancing at his Rolex watch, then back up at the drama. He, along with everyone else, looked as if they were watching a train wreck so awful, yet so captivating, that they couldn't stand to tear themselves away.

"I still need to make two important phone calls this evening," he continued reluctantly. "I think I've sufficiently done my duty and made my appearance here. I guess I should slip out while everyone is distracted by all the commotion."

Phillip paused, then nodded toward the suspects and continued almost hesitantly. "Could you do me a favor, Rachel? I know you can't tell me classified information, but if you could just tell me something of what happens, I would really appreciate it."

Rachel had no idea why Phillip was still being so nice and polite to her. His usual behavior would be to demand right now that she tell him what was going on. After what her dad had told her, she was already very angry with her brother, and it was difficult to not fly off the handle and give him the lecture that would at least make her feel better. Rachel fully intended on confronting Phillip about the ranch and their dad, but now was not the time or place.

"I'll see what I can do," Rachel said simply. She'd have to talk to Dawson and possibly Andrews. It would probably be worth it to tell him something that would satisfy his curiosity and concern, just so he would leave her alone.

"Thanks. I'll see you later."

Rachel gave a distracted wave, still focused on searching the room for some danger or clue they had missed. The guests turned to each other to begin their gossip as the men finally exited the room and headed toward the transport vehicles. There were already plenty of police and agents surrounding their progress. Other security stood at the door, preventing them from being followed.

The danger was over, right? The ring leader of a powerful terrorist ring should have plenty of backup for an important exchange like this. Should she be on the alert for some rescue attempt? Rachel didn't know how many participants the other team had already apprehended with the bomb. At this point, though, it seemed unlikely that their suspects would receive help from any reinforcements.

Rachel's gaze slid across the large windows at the front of the ballroom. Entering though the window wouldn't be an option. The hotel was surrounded by security, police, and government agents. Plus, crashing through windows wouldn't exactly be subtle. No, if there were other terrorists, they would have to be already inside.

Rachel froze. Something clicked in her mind. She suddenly realized why she was so unsettled. Moreover, she knew what had bothered her about Amir's murder.

The epiphany quickly morphed into a sickening realization as the final grotesque puzzle piece slid firmly into place. With it, so many other details and events suddenly made sense. It was as if she had been looking through a pair of severely distorted glasses that had suddenly been removed, allowing her to see clearly for the first time. The effect was overwhelming. The ramifications— almost unbearable.

She had to be wrong. There had to be another explanation. There was no way she was right. It was impossible.

Whirling around, Rachel took off in the opposite direction from her coworkers. She rapidly swerved through guests, her heart pounding a firm denial of what her mind had already decided on as a certainty. Pushing open the door to the ballroom, she ran to the elevator. She waited impatiently for each number on the overhead display to light up as the elevator approached. She knew that, in her gown and heels, the elevator would still be faster than the stairs. At the elevator's friendly ding of arrival, Rachel rushed in and pushed the button for the lowest level—the hotel parking garage. Thankfully, there were no other passengers, and after descending, the doors slid open to the dark, cement cavern.

Rachel rushed out, frantically looking all directions through the dim light. She saw him.

"Phillip!" she called, her voice sounding strangled and out of breath. Evidently hearing her feeble call, he turned as she rushed up, her heels echoing a staccato rhythm across the concrete.

"What's wrong, Rachel?" he asked, his voice laced with concern.

Rachel stopped about eight feet in front of her brother. She stared at him, examining every feature of the face she already knew so well. She watched as a light dawned on his face and the concern was replaced by a confident, wry half-smile.

"What's wrong, Rachel?" he asked again, but this time, his tone almost held a note of amusement.

"Amir's murderer didn't enter from outside," she finally responded. "He had to have already been inside the room."

Rachel's voice was thoughtful as she studied every small muscle change in Phillip's stone-like face. "If he'd entered from the outside, Amir would have heard him and called out. Even with glass cutting tools, Amir would have heard him coming. He had to have hidden in the room, hit Amir with a dart so he wouldn't sound a warning, and then executed him. He cut the window glass and disabled the lock after the murder to make it appear as if an intruder had entered. Then he left by way of that same window."

"Sounds like you have it all figured out," Phillip replied with a smile, "but why are you telling your theory to me?"

"Remember how we played hide and seek when we were young? I was only about 5. It was before you decided you didn't like me. One of our favorite hiding places was behind the shelving unit in the spare room closet. It was always positioned far enough from the wall to allow us to sneak behind it. I bet it's large enough that even an adult could fit back there. That closet itself is at the back of the room, on the wall to the right of the window. It would have been relatively easy for the murderer to hide in there, then come out and hit Amir in the back with a dart before he had a chance to call out."

Phillip was silent, his expression revealing nothing.

"You got the room ready," Rachel continued. "You were the only other one in the house who knew about that closet. It was you, wasn't it? It was you who killed Amir."

Phillip didn't respond, the slight smile on his face never changing.

"You're the boss, aren't you," Rachel whispered. "New York. Everything. It's all been you."

Rachel heard the unmistakable sound of a gun cocking and felt the pressure of a barrel against the back of her head.

"Hello, Rachel," purred an all-too familiar voice.

Chapter 20

"Hello, Vanessa," Rachel answered calmly without even moving her head. "It's nice to finally meet my brother's girlfriend, though I almost didn't recognize you in your waitress disguise."

"Oh, I'm touched," Vanessa Riley replied. "I didn't think you'd even remember, let alone recognize me."

In all honesty, Rachel hadn't recognized John Riley's only child until the moment she had realized the truth about Phillip: he had to have been the one to murder Amir. With that single epiphany, Rachel saw the entire, complicated picture and realized exactly who the pretty blond waitress was. The other waiter had been a decoy. Vanessa had purposely bumped into him and exchanged the schematics in the resulting confusion. Then both she and Phillip had waited until the natural, perfect moment to make their exit. Dawson had been right. Vanessa Riley was an incredible actress.

"Do you have what we need, Vanessa?" Phillip asked.

"Of course," Vanessa responded.

Rachel knew they were referring to the schematics for their terrorist plot. The exchange had been successful.

"I guess your friend Amir didn't mention the fact that there are two bombs," Phillip sneered. "Oh, that's right, he only knew about the one. I have to hand it to you though, Rachel, I thought I had gotten to him before he had a chance to talk. Obviously, I was wrong. You and your friends have definitely made things more difficult here tonight, but I really only need one bomb. The other one was just for insurance anyway."

Rachel stared, unbelieving, at her brother. Until that moment, she had held out hope that this was some big mistake. Maybe it was all Vanessa Riley and Phillip was just a pawn. But no. Rachel felt nauseous. This had all been orchestrated by Phillip Saunders, her only sibling.

"Search her, Vanessa," Phillip ordered. "I already know she's not transmitting. Our men have confirmed that. But you need to check for weapons."

Rachel choked down the emotion. She had to maintain focus if she was going to get out of this alive. It hadn't even occurred to her to call for backup before confronting Phillip. Now she was very much regretting her hasty actions.

Trying to keep her confident facade in place, Rachel spoke to Vanessa. "Dawson will be so relieved that you haven't been pining for him. Although he will be disappointed to know you were involved with the terrorist ring all along. He said he could never find any evidence against you."

"That's because there was none," Vanessa said as she began patting Rachel down with one hand, holding the gun with the other. "I knew about all of my dad's business dealings, but he wouldn't let me be involved in his more risky endeavors. After his arrest, though, I took over everything. Phillip and I finally met, and I guess you could say we have developed some mutually beneficial arrangements."

Vanessa's hand was patting down Rachel's back. Rachel had to think of something fast. She didn't want Vanessa finding the gun she had concealed on her leg.

Not only had she been foolish to confront Phillip alone, she had also come down here with the gun on her leg as her only weapon. However, in her defense, a girl didn't normally anticipate being held at gunpoint by her brother and his girlfriend.

Vanessa wasn't really paying attention to the gun in her other hand. It wouldn't be difficult to disarm her and take her down. If she just…

"Don't even think about it, Rachel," Phillip said, a gun appearing in his own hand. He deliberately brought it up and leveled it at his sister. "I know you're fully capable of taking Vanessa down, but if you try anything, you'll be dead before you touch her gun. I may not have trained with Dad like you, but I know how you think and what you can do. Trust me; at this range, I don't need to be an expert shot."

"And you obviously have no problem with killing your sister," Rachel said, angered and completely disgusted. "After all, it's not like you haven't tried to kill me before."

"I'm not as cold-hearted as you think, Rachel," Phillip said, his expression seeming genuinely troubled and sincere. "I never wanted you to be killed or harmed in any way."

"I find that hard to believe. You arranged for me to be the mule for the bomb in New York almost a year ago! What did you expect to happen?"

"That wasn't me. It was John Riley. I specifically told him I didn't want you involved. He made the arrangements without my knowledge."

If she could just keep them talking, maybe she could find an escape. Phillip was still about eight feet away with his gun pointed directly at her. There was no way she could incapacitate both Vanessa and Phillip without getting shot.

"I don't believe you," Rachel retorted. "I heard how Amir and the others talked about you. According to them, you are a ruthless micro-manager. How could you not know?"

Completing her thorough search of Rachel's person, Vanessa stood back up, having already removed the Walther 9mm that had been strapped to Rachel's leg.

Instead of Phillip, Vanessa answered the question. "Phillip was supposed to have gained complete control of your family's ranch so our headquarters could be safely located there. When that didn't happen, we still managed to get things built there in the shack, but my dad was always worried you would stumble across it. He tried to convince Phillip that if you were eliminated, the threat would be gone and the ranch would fall to him, eliminating all our problems. When Phillip refused, Dad realized Phillip was too emotionally involved to make the right call, so Dad took matters into his own hands. It was pretty simple to arrange for you to win an all-expense paid trip to New York.

You were supposed to carry that bomb into the hotel and be out of the picture before Phillip even realized what Dad had done."

"Needless to say, I wasn't happy when I did find out," Phillip said. "John wanted to finish the job and have you eliminated even after New York, but I wouldn't let him."

Vanessa smirked. "Dad told me you actually told him that if something happened to your sister, you'd make sure something happened to his daughter."

"I wanted to keep you safe, Rachel," Phillip said, anger now lacing his voice. "If Dad would have just listened to me in the very beginning, we could have sold the ranch to a fake company and had you and the rest of the family move away. Then you and our parents would have been safe and we would have had legitimate access to the secluded area we needed. But Dad wouldn't listen to any of my options. Then when you finally did find the shack, everything changed. From that point on, I knew you'd have to die."

"But you didn't kill me," Rachel argued, hoping that her brother still had enough affection for her that she could reach through his twisted mind. "The men at the shack said you wouldn't let them kill me. You could have just done it at the ranch and not even bothered kidnapping me, but you didn't. You were the one who shot me with the dart, weren't you? And then you must have had Lou beat you up to make it appear that you were a victim too."

Phillip grimaced. "At that point, I was still trying to find a way so I wouldn't have to kill you. You forced me to reveal myself to Lou. Then I had to cover my tracks so I wouldn't seem like a suspect. I told Lou he had to make it look real, but I didn't necessarily count on getting a concussion out of it."

"You insisted the men at the shack use darts on me, not lethal force. Amir really wanted to kill me, but all of them knew you wouldn't let him. I'm your sister, Phillip. You haven't committed a terrorist act yet. Please, let me help you. You weren't going to kill me then. And I don't think you will now."

Phillip smirked. "Now you've switched sides, Rachel. You're thinking way too highly of me. I don't have a problem killing you now. As I said, you've left me no choice. I tried to figure out a way to save you, but I couldn't. I've already ordered your death once. In a sense, the dye has been cast. I certainly won't have a problem pulling the trigger now."

"What do you mean, you ordered my death?"

"Amir didn't contact me after the shack was destroyed. I contacted him. I told him to kill you. Of course, he had his own reasons for wanting you dead and was only too willing to comply. I developed the plan and told him exactly how to do it. I hired the decoy to enter your room to provide a distraction so Amir could get close. I told him where to find mom, though I certainly wouldn't have let him kill her. Mom was just supposed to be leverage to get you to cooperate. Those men attacked Aunt Mary's house following Amir's instructions, not mine. If your friend hadn't killed them, I would have hunted them down myself. Unfortunately, that wasn't the only part of the plan Amir screwed up. He couldn't manage to kill you but got himself captured instead. So of course, I had to silence him before he was transferred and interrogated. So you see, Rachel, I'd already decided you needed to die. In my mind, your death warrant has already been signed."

Rachel felt the blood drain from her face, not as much from what Phillip had said as from the memory his words triggered. With goose bumps prickling the back of her neck, Rachel recalled John Riley's quiet snarl, *"I should have killed you when I had the chance. You have no idea, do you? Life is just a crazy coincidence? That's fine. I have a feeling even mercy has a limit."*

The words she had struggled to shrug off as the ramblings of a psychopath, now made sense.

Riley had been talking about her brother. He had wanted to kill her in New York or soon afterwards, but Phillip hadn't let him. Had she now reached the limit of Phillip's mercy?

"If you would have had the decency to die back in New York, we wouldn't be having this problem," Vanessa grumbled.

"Get her in the car, Vanessa," Phillip said, glancing at his watch. "We need to get out of here before she's missed."

"Phillip?" Rachel whispered.

Her brother looked her straight in the eye, his expression completely dead. There was no love, not even a flicker of emotion.

Vanessa propelled her toward the car while Phillip followed with his gun. Rachel knew she should fight. She shouldn't get in the car but should make her stand here, no matter what the outcome. But a mind-numbing sorrow had completely engulfed her. She couldn't think, let alone make her limbs obey her wishes.

Each step felt as if it was in slow motion. Memories flashed through her mind of growing up with Phillip. Funny how she was remembering only the good times. Interlaced through each of those pictures was the brutal pain of what Phillip had become and what he was about to do. How could this be happening?

Phillip was going to kill her.

They arrived at Phillip's car. He unlocked it and reached for the door handle, his body freezing at the sound of a voice.

"That's far enough, Son."

Rachel peered around Vanessa to see her father with grief-stricken blue eyes and a revolver, both trained on Phillip.

Chapter 21

Rachel didn't know how much of the conversation her dad had heard, but by the tortured look on his face, she knew he'd heard enough to figure things out.

His eyes locked with Phillip's for a long moment.

Finally, he spoke quietly. "Phillip let your sister go."

"Sorry, Dad, I can't do that." Phillip's confident sneer appeared once again. "But really, the only one you have to blame for this is yourself. If you would have just sold the ranch when I told you to, this wouldn't have happened. Rachel wouldn't have found our operation, and no one would have been the wiser. If you hadn't insisted the whole ranch go completely to Rachel, maybe this wouldn't have happened. If you would have let me have some sway in the management of the ranch, I could have found a way to protect her. But you did none of that. You've left me no choice now."

"You always have a choice," Dad said, his voice still quiet, gentle, sincere. "All of your choices have led you to this point. You decided to be this man. And that's what I don't understand. Why, Phillip? Why?"

"It's not personal, Dad. It's just business. You have no idea what we're doing. I'm sure you think my actions appear reprehensible. But when someone offers you more money and power than you ever dreamed, you don't refuse. We are not plotting against our own people. Our plan will do things for this country that could be achieved in no other way. To some, I'd be considered a patriot."

"There's nothing patriotic about killing defenseless people, especially your own countrymen. That's just murder and treason."

"You see it your way, and I see it mine. How is that different from everything else my entire life?"

Rachel closed her eyes briefly. *God, please help us!* She did not see this ending well. She would never understand Phillip or the reasons behind his actions. But she did know that hunger for power and money, coupled with a twisted ideology, could lead anyone to do horrific acts. She also knew that there was no reasoning with such a person.

"I can't let you do this," her dad said, apparently also realizing that trying to rationalize with Phillip would be pointless. "And I won't let you harm your sister. Let her go and turn yourself in peacefully."

"Sorry, Dad, that's not going to happen."

"Don't make me stop you, Son."

Phillip smirked. "I know you, Dad. There's no way you're going to put a bullet in your own son. I'm going to get in the car and leave with Rachel while you stand there helplessly holding your gun and wondering what you did wrong for your son to be such a monster. As much as you'd like to, you're not going to stop me."

"Well, if Carson doesn't put a bullet in you, I will," Dawson appeared a few yards to Carson's left. His Glock was drawn and already focused on his target. "I certainly don't have an ethical problem with killing you, Phillip."

"Don't worry, Dawson," came Garrett's voice as he appeared a few yards to Carson's right. "If you take care of Phillip, I'll take care of your pretty ex-fiancé over there. By the way, Vanessa, you definitely need to lose the blond wig. Blond looks much better on Rachel than you. Carson, since we have both of them covered, maybe you could add a bullet to each of them for good measure? Phillip, if I were you, I wouldn't ever underestimate your dad. Son or not, he'll do what needs to be done."

Silence stretched for several heartbeats as the tension grew almost unbearable.

She felt Phillip slide his hand down to his pocket, but it was at an angle the other men couldn't see. What was he doing? He already had a gun in his other hand. She heard a strange beep as if he had pushed a button on a cell phone or just received a text message.

"You're outnumbered, Phillip," Carson said. "Put down your weapon and let Rachel go."

"Sorry, Dad." With a quick motion, Phillip yanked Rachel over, put his arm tightly around her, and firmly placed the muzzle of his gun into her temple. "Rachel just became my insurance policy."

His voice deadly calm, Phillip outlined his plan. "Vanessa is going to drive while I keep my gun in this happy place against Rachel's head. If anyone attempts to stop or follow us, I will pull the trigger. I think you all know I don't have a problem with killing her and won't hesitate a single second. If instead, we get away safely, I will let her live while Vanessa and I disappear where you'll never find us. Does everyone understand?"

The next few seconds passed as if each one was the frame of a movie in slow motion. As all three men slowly nodded their understanding, Rachel made eye contact with Dawson. She was not going to get in the car. She could never trust Phillip. He would kill her even if they did follow his instructions to the letter. With just that brief glance, Rachel communicated her wishes to Dawson. They had discussed this very scenario. She was not going to be used as a weapon or a hostage. It didn't matter that it was her brother threatening her life. Dawson had promised to take the shot.

Rachel's mind flashed back to her conversation with Dawson after her kidnapping. That experience had changed things for him, and he had almost seemed to retract his promise. Would he even be able to emotionally handle taking the shot? There was very little margin for error. If his aim was off even a little, he would hit Rachel. If he missed or was late pulling the trigger, Phillip would pull his trigger and kill her.

Rachel pushed her frantic thoughts aside. She searched Dawson's eyes from across the yards separating them. She saw a brief flash of panic, then read his acceptance. Dawson would take the shot. He had to.

Moving her gaze to the left, she met her dad's eyes. She tried to wordlessly communicate the plan. Her dad was the one who had always told her to do whatever it takes, but never get in the car. Surprisingly, she read an intensity in his gaze that even now was demanding that she fight. With an almost imperceptible nod, Rachel signaled that she understood. If Dawson couldn't take the shot, she had no doubt that her dad would do it himself. As for Garrett, she had to trust that he would follow their lead and take care of Vanessa.

The first move was hers. She just had to get away enough to let Dawson get a clear angle. He would be going for the kill shot. It's what they were trained to do. Her mind spun rapidly through different options. Dawson and her dad expected her to just get out of the way, but maybe if she took Phillip down herself, she could save his life.

God, help me! Despite everything he's done, I don't want my brother to die!

Before she had time to decide on the right technique, she felt Phillip's arm leave its grip on her as it opened the car door. Now was the only chance she was going to get.

She subtly moved her body back toward the car door, making it difficult for Phillip to open. She felt Phillip push her forward with his hand, trying to get her out of the way. At the pressure on her back, Rachel moved forward just as he expected, but then she swung around quickly, turning to face Phillip and the gun. Her left arm rose, knocking his gun hand up. Simultaneously, she reached up with her right hand, grabbing the gun from underneath. As her left hand pulled on his wrist, her right twisted the weapon out of his faltering grip. Quickly, she swung the gun back in a downward angle with all her strength and momentum, striking Phillip hard on the forehead, aiming at a point high and a little left of center. His knees instantly buckled, and he crumpled to the ground unconscious.

Though Rachel's movements had been so rapid Phillip couldn't have even processed what was happening, shots had rung out the instant Rachel had swung around. In the brief seconds it took to take Phillip down, Rachel was vaguely aware that there were more shots than she expected, and some of them seemed to be coming from the wrong direction.

As Phillip went down, Rachel heard a gun fire at close range, even as she felt the impact of the bullet. She had been shot.

Chapter 22

Reacting instinctively, Rachel whirled to face her attacker, Phillip's gun now firmly in her grip. With no pause in motion, Rachel brought the gun up and squeezed the trigger three times in rapid succession. Three bullets hit their targets. Disbelief registered in Vanessa's eyes right before she collapsed to the concrete.

Rachel turned all directions, weapon at the ready, senses on high alert. She heard the popping sound of more gunshots, a pause, and then one last single shot. The garage was then filled with an eerie, oppressive silence. The firefight was over mere seconds after it had begun.

Rachel glanced down at the blood seeping from her left shoulder. She'd been shot, yet strangely, she didn't feel the pain. It looked as if the bullet had passed cleanly from back to front, exiting without causing lethal damage.

Vanessa began screaming. Her cries of pain intermingled with curses directed at Rachel, echoing off the walls of the parking garage.

Rachel ignored her, still straining to identify signs of danger. Though she couldn't see Garrett, she could vaguely hear his voice on his phone, urgently requesting assistance. She spotted her dad standing behind a pillar near the wall, his Colt revolver at the ready. Across from him and directly in front of her, Dawson scurried between two cars, his body small and hunched over.

She saw Dawson look over at her dad. Carson shook his head at some unspoken question and held up three fingers. Dawson straightened a little and pivoted, scanning the area with his gun in firing position.

Over the hood of a car, his eyes met Rachel's. Rachel saw a bolt of intensity flash through his eyes.

She froze.

Dawson aimed his gun directly at her head... and fired.

She heard the sound of something large falling. Turning quickly, she saw Dawson had shot someone standing behind her, on the other side of Phillip's car. With the impact of the bullet, the attacker's body had slumped onto the rear of car beside Phillip's BMW and was now sliding off onto the ground.

"And that would be Bad Guy Number 3," Carson said, now moving confidently away from the pillar.

"You're sure there were only three?" Dawson asked cautiously, still nervously surveying the area with gun drawn. "This garage has a really bad echo for trying to figure out where bullets are coming from."

"Only three gunmen," Carson confirmed. "Bullets came from three directions. They were all using different weapons, which have a slightly different sound when firing. I got fairly good at figuring that sort of thing out in my Army sniper days."

"What happened?" Rachel asked as Dawson walked toward her, but instead of coming directly to her, he went around the BMW, bent, and checked the body of the gunman.

"Phillip had his own backup," Dawson answered. "When you moved, three other gunmen opened fire on us. Thankfully, either they weren't very good shots or they were distracted by watching you take down their boss. Phillip probably had them waiting to make sure he got out of here. My guess is that they would have been ordered to kill us the second he left this parking garage.

Rachel now understood what Phillip had been doing with his phone. He'd been giving a signal for his backup to move into position.

Garrett and her dad walked up, right as Dawson straightened from his inspection.

"He's dead," Dawson announced.

"So are the other two," Garrett confirmed as he bent over Phillip, who was still unconscious beside Rachel. Turning him over, Garrett pulled his arms back and secured them with a pair of handcuffs. "How long is he going to be out?"

"Probably another fifteen minutes," Rachel said.

"I guess we don't really need to handcuff her," Garrett said, gesturing toward Vanessa. "It's not like she can go anywhere. We should be getting help, including an ambulance, at any minute."

Though Rachel had effectively tuned Vanessa out, she now became aware that the injured woman was still crying and screaming obscenities. Her eyes were filled with hatred and focused on Rachel as she thrashed.

"Vanessa, you should lie still," Dawson instructed. "You're going to be fine, but you'll lose more blood if you keep struggling."

"I'm going to be fine? She shot me three times! I'll probably never be able to walk or use my arms again! I am NOT going to be fine!" Vanessa followed her tirade up with a string of angry curses.

"Vanessa, stop it!" Dawson ordered firmly. "You should be thanking Rachel. She apparently didn't feel like killing you today. Rachel doesn't miss. She put bullets in your arms so you couldn't shoot and a leg so you couldn't run. Just be thankful she decided to use three bullets instead of one."

"I would have just used one," Garrett grumbled.

Rachel was quiet. Strictly speaking, she should have taken the kill shot. That's what she had been trained to do. Vanessa had already taken the first shot. She knew the only way to completely incapacitate an attacker was to kill her. But, in the split second she had turned around and saw Vanessa a few feet away holding the gun, she hadn't wanted to kill her. She knew she wasn't injured badly, and she knew that Vanessa was not a trained operative. So she disregarded her training and attempted mercy with a shot to each shoulder and one to the leg.

As multiple cars and two ambulances screeched onto the garage, police and other agents rushed onto the scene, and Dawson turned to really look at Rachel for the first time. His eyes, filled with respect and sympathy, suddenly flew wide.

"Rachel, were you shot?"

Rachel looked down at the blood rolling down her left arm and felt a little dizzy.

"Vanessa got a shot off before I could finish with Phillip. It's nothing. The bullet passed clean through my shoulder. Though I doubt I'll be able to salvage my dress."

Ignoring Rachel's attempt at humor, Dawson wordlessly lifted her up and carried her to a nearby ambulance.

"Put me down, Dawson! I am fully capable of walking!"

"Montana, you are as white as a sheet and surely in shock. There's no telling how much blood you've lost. Just humor me until the paramedics check you out."

As soon as Dawson set her on the back of the ambulance, two paramedics immediately made her lie down inside and began treating her wound. They repeatedly checked her vital signs, started an IV, and cleaned and bandaged the wound with thick pads.

Dawson had been called away to help deal with the investigation. Phillip had already been loaded into a transport vehicle. Not willing to take any chances, Garrett was to personally accompany

Phillip to a secure location. Vanessa had already been loaded into the ambulance, which was readying to leave momentarily.

"Am I done?" Rachel asked impatiently, seeing that the bag of fluids attached to her IV was now empty.

"No, this is just a temporary fix to get you to the hospital," one of the paramedics answered firmly. "You'll probably not need surgery, but you do need to be treated by a doctor and get some good pain medication. When the shock wears off, you're going to be in a lot of pain. We can leave as soon as we get the go ahead saying the area is secure."

"Thanks," Rachel said, sitting up. "I'll head to the hospital as soon as possible, but I can't go right now. Could you please remove the IV?"

The paramedics pinned her with an incredulous look. "You can refuse treatment if you want, but I would strongly advise against it. You need to stay still until a doctor can examine you."

Rachel had to get out of there. She was worried about her dad and couldn't tolerate sitting a minute longer. She hadn't seen him since the first few moments after Dawson shot the third gunman. He hadn't even been there when Dawson had figured out she'd been shot.

"I've been watching you," Rachel said, feeling desperate to leave. "My vital signs are fine, right? I promise I'll get to the hospital within the hour, but I really can't right now. Do you want to remove the IV or can I just do it myself?"

The reluctant, grumbling paramedic finally removed the IV and positioned her arm in a sling to keep it immobile.

Rachel hurried away before he could do anything other than protest. Knowing Dawson would throw a fit if he saw her ducking out on further medical treatment, Rachel carefully avoided him and walked down the line of parked cars, moving away from the other people.

Where was her dad? He wasn't with Dawson or Garrett, and he didn't seem to be helping any other agents with the investigation. That wasn't like him.

Finally, at the end of the row, hidden in a dark corner, Rachel found Carson Saunders.

He was kneeling as if in prayer, his gun on the cement beside him.

"Dad?" Rachel questioned. As she neared, she saw his shoulders shaking convulsively. She knelt beside him, gently wrapping her good arm around him.

Bending, she caught a glimpse of his down-turned face. His features were twisted in agony as tears coursed down, and his body was wracked with quiet, heartbreaking sobs.

Gathering him close, Rachel leaned her cheek next to his. Only then could she understand his softly whispered, gut-wrenching moans.

"My son… my son!"

*****

Dawson was speaking with Andrews as Rachel approached. Not wanting to interrupt, she held back a little. The pain in her shoulder had hit while she was with her dad. Now it was excruciating. She didn't feel like answering twenty questions from her boss right now. She just wanted to talk to Dawson and find someone to drive her to the hospital.

Trying to focus on anything other than the pain, her mind locked onto the conversation between Dawson and Andrews, especially when she caught her own name.

"Rachel is the one who deserves the credit," Dawson was saying. "If I had just done my job and figured out Phillip was our guy, none of this would have happened."

Andrews shook his head. "You know you checked him out early on along with everyone else close to Rachel. There was no evidence. No red flags. Don't be too hard on yourself, Tate. You're hands-down the best undercover agent I have. This has been a long case. You've been working this Montana angle for what, a year now? You should be relieved it's over. Now you can get back to your own life."

What was he talking about? Rachel thought, becoming increasingly agitated. Before Rachel had found the shack, Dawson hadn't known there was a Montana connection to the attempted bombing in New York. He had always told her it was random.

Dawson's eyes flew wide as he caught sight of Rachel standing behind Andrews.

"Rachel!" he said, obviously startled. His face seemed to pale under the dim overhead lights.

At Dawson's cry, Andrews turned around, his expression wary. Quickly recovering, Andrews smoothed his features and addressed Rachel. "Saunders, why aren't you at the hospital? Tate said you were shot."

"It's not a bad injury," Rachel replied, a little startled by Andrews' harsh, business-like tone. Usually he was very warm and pleasant to her. "I'll head to the hospital as soon as I can get someone to give me a ride."

"I'll assign an agent to take you right now," he said. "You cannot be here. You're too close to the situation. We can't risk even the suspicion of evidence tampering. I'm taking you completely off the case. Go get patched up at the hospital. As soon as they release you, we'll book you on a flight to New York. Tate will stay here to wrap up the investigation. I've already sent men to your house to search Phillip's room there. But I can't risk having you anywhere near this until it's completely wrapped up."

Rachel's mind was spinning as she tried to keep up with all of the information Andrews was throwing at her. She could understand being taken off the case, but he was sending her back to New York?

"Where is your dad?" Andrews asked, turning around, as if expecting to see him. "He can't be around here either."

"He already left," Rachel said. "He was driving directly to my Aunt Mary's house to meet my mom. He wanted to break the news about Phillip to her in person."

"But that's three hours away!" Dawson said. "How is he doing? Is he okay to drive?"

Rachel shrugged. "He's having a hard time, but there was no talking him out of it. Driving has always been therapeutic for my dad, so I think he'll be fine. He didn't even stop at the ranch to get clothes or anything. He wanted to reach my mom before she heard the news some other way."

Rachel had sat with her dad for a long time, her own tears flowing in their mutual grief. They hadn't said much. Rachel hadn't offered words of comfort, for she knew that no platitudes could touch the pain her dad was feeling. She herself had yet to process everything that had happened with her brother. Her tears were more for her grief-stricken father.

Carson had eventually gained control and become focused on what needed to be done. He knew he had to get to Rachel's mom and had to be strong for her.

Rachel had never seen her father sob like that, and she doubted she ever would again. The moment was over. The initial shock and horror of what Phillip had done was traumatic. Deep down, though, Rachel knew Carson Saunders would be okay. He was a strong man, but Rachel knew the source of his strength. And she had full confidence that God would comfort and take care of her daddy as no one else could.

So she had waved as he had driven away in his truck. Only afterward had she realized that her dad had never even noticed that she had been shot. It was kind of hard to miss the blue sling and large white bandage across her left shoulder, but Rachel was just thankful he had been too focused and distracted to really see her appearance. If he had, he probably would have insisted on staying with her.

"Good," Andrews was saying. "I'll give him a call tomorrow and let him know that he'll need to stay away for a few days while we wrap things up. I'm headed back to New York myself as soon as we're done at the scene here. I'll be better able to facilitate all the angles of this case from there. Wait right here, Saunders. I'll send an agent with a car to take you to the hospital."

As Andrews walked away, Rachel turned to Dawson.

"What did Andrews mean about you investigating the 'Montana connection,'" she wasted no time in asking.

Dawson shrugged and looked away from her as if he were intensely interested in a group of agents standing by the elevators, blocking both people and cars from entering this level. By now, the party had ended and guests were anxious to get to their vehicles.

"You know Andrews," he replied. "He just meant that it's been almost a year since that initial attempted bombing in New York. Now we've finally found the origin of that incident, and we'll be able to close the case, confident we've found those responsible."

Rachel didn't buy it. His explanation was so simple it made no sense. Added to that was the fact Dawson didn't seem to want to look her in the eye.

With a sense of dread, Rachel realized she recognized this feeling. She had experienced it before, but Dawson had promised her it would never happen again. Now, despite his promises, her boyfriend was hiding something from her once again. She felt dizzy and suddenly, almost overwhelmingly sick to her stomach. For with a horrible certainty, she knew what was wrong. Dawson Tate was lying.

Chapter 23

Rachel opened the desk drawer and shuffled quickly through its contents. This wasn't the first time she had searched through Dawson's things, but this time was different. She wasn't bothering to be neat or unobtrusive. She really didn't care if he knew she had torn apart his room searching. He had lied to her, and she was going to find out the truth.

Frustrated, she slammed the desk drawer shut. Nothing. She had already gone through nearly every item in the ranch guest house where Dawson stayed.

When she had searched his rooms before, Dawson was missing and she had been looking for any kind of clue to his whereabouts. Now she knew a lot more about how to do a thorough search than she did back then, and this time, she knew exactly what she was looking for. Dawson always kept a failsafe on the cases he was working. If he was working on a case involving her, he would have kept files detailing his investigation, and he would have kept them close.

But she was running out of time. It had taken a lot longer at the hospital than she had anticipated. The doctor had packed her wound with some kind of gel to help it heal and rebandaged it. Although her wound wasn't serious and wouldn't require surgery, the doctor was concerned that her body was still experiencing shock. He had wanted her to stay at the hospital at least the rest of the night for observation. She had refused. In the end, he had grudgingly released her after prescribing two kinds of pain medication—one that would make her intensely drowsy and one that would not.

Although they had given her medication prior to dressing the wound, Rachel was still in so much pain she was shaking. She took the non-drowsy pain medicine, but it only seemed to take the edge off. The doctor had said the other kind was stronger, but Rachel couldn't risk taking it yet and having it knock her out. She needed to stay alert for a while yet.

Rachel glanced at her watch. It was 3:00 in the morning. She had orders to be on a flight to New York in three hours.

Andrews had been completely serious when he said they would book her on a flight to New York upon her release from the hospital. Not five minutes after exiting the hospital doors, Kelsey was calling with flight information. Since she was unable to drive with her injury, Andrews had assigned the same agent who took her to the hospital to continue as her taxi. She was to go home to pack her things and then make it to the airport for her flight. But Rachel knew her escort's real assignment was to keep an eye on her, especially when she was at home.

The pain and stress made her feel as if every nerve in her body was vibrating. She had to find that file! She had already taken too long searching. The agent that had been assigned to her would come looking for her if she didn't show up soon.

Andrews had already said he couldn't risk even the suspicion that the investigation had been compromised in any way. As if she would tamper with any evidence to try to help her terrorist brother who had kidnapped and tried to have her killed! Regardless, she understood Andrews' caution, if only for the sake of appearances. She hadn't argued with his plan.

He really should have assigned a better agent to her though. It had been way too easy to ditch him. After cleaning up and packing some of her things for New York, she had told him that she needed to check on and feed the animals, maybe even muck the manure out of a few stalls before she left. She had thoughtfully invited him to join her, but the agent, thoroughly appalled at the thought, had said he would just wait for her inside.

She had actually done as she said and checked on and fed some of the animals, but she knew Xavier would come in a few hours to finish the work. He was qualified enough to take care of everything while she and her dad were away.

It had been very easy to slip away from her chores undetected and take a detour to the guest house to search Dawson's things. Unfortunately, she knew that her inept friend would eventually conquer his aversion and come looking for her if she didn't show up soon.

Rachel's thoughts spun around like flies around a horse. Though the doctor and everyone else had encouraged her to get some rest, she hadn't slept a wink and was probably in both physical and emotional shock. Where would Dawson put that file? She leaned back in the desk chair, shut her eyes, and tried to focus her tired mind.

Maybe she shouldn't be looking for a physical paper file. That would be too large and obvious. If he had really been working some mystery case for almost a year, the file would be absolutely huge. Dawson was meticulous at keeping detailed notes.

Plus, Dawson knew she was naturally nosy. She had already searched his things once, and he probably at least half expected her to do it again. There's no way he'd leave something obvious like that laying around.

It was possible that Dawson kept the file in some other location, but she didn't think it likely. He had used a safety deposit box to conceal his case files before, but there wasn't a bank close to the ranch where he could do that. It wasn't like Dawson to use the exact same method twice anyway. No, he would keep the file close at hand, but it would have to be small, maybe something digital. She had already searched his desktop computer. No surprise, he didn't have any work- related files on there. He mainly seemed to use it for doing case research and browsing the Internet. She'd already searched every book on his shelves and even pulled frames off the walls to look inside. She had found no CD or other device to store information. She had also carefully inspected each piece of furniture, but hadn't found any secret compartment.

Rachel focused on what the file would look like. It would have to be small, probably portable, and appear so ordinary someone looking wouldn't give it a second glance.

She opened her eyes and sat up. She turned her seat in a full circle, trying to assess everything with this new criteria. Finally, her gaze ended back at the desk. She once again opened the drawers. There were two drawers to the right. Bills were in the top while miscellaneous office supplies were in the lower one. The wide, shallow one directly above her knees held mostly pens and pencils. She rummaged through them idly, finally picking up the nicest pen in the hodgepodge variety. It was big and heavy, looking more expensive than the others. She looked for some kind of emblem or business name, wondering where Dawson had gotten such a nice pen, but there was nothing.

In a moment of sheer inspiration, Rachel pulled at the barrel of the pen. It popped off easily in her hand, now just a simple, hollow plastic cylinder. Her heart leapt as she stared at the heavy part of the pen still in her left hand. Attached to the normal ballpoint writing section was a long, narrow computer memory card. The barrel of the pen had fit so neatly and perfectly over the top, it had very effectively hidden the device.

This was what she was looking for! It had to be! She quickly removed the card from the pen and inserted it into Dawson's computer. She drummed her fingers on the desk impatiently as the computer took its time opening the files.

Finally, clicking on a file labeled 'Montana,' Dawson's case notes appeared on the screen. The start date for the case was listed as the date of the attempted bombing in New York last fall. Right below that was a brief description of Dawson's assignment, especially as it related to the asset he was to utilize to obtain the needed information.

The asset was identified as Rachel Saunders.

And that was the moment Rachel's entire world fell apart.

Chapter 24

Rachel lightly tossed the memory card across the desk. It skidded to a stop right in front of Dawson.

She saw instant recognition cross Dawson's features as he looked at the device. His face turned ashen beneath his normally tanned skin. He swallowed and looked up, his eyes meeting Rachel's.

"Garrett, could you excuse us a minute?" Dawson asked quietly.

At Rachel's request, her agent escort had willingly brought her to the temporary headquarters for investigating this case. Finding Garrett and Dawson working in a back office, she had entered the room unexpected and unannounced.

After glancing between Rachel and Dawson, Garrett was surprisingly compliant and left the room wordlessly. As he left, he shot Rachel a look of sympathy and understanding. Had he known about Dawson's investigation?

As the door shut softly, Dawson spoke, "Rachel, I can explain."

"You can explain?" Rachel retorted, her voice soft yet tight with seething anger. "Explain that our relationship has been a lie from the very beginning? Explain that you were assigned to me so that you could use me to try to find the source of the New York terrorist attack?

Dawson groaned, bending his head over the desk and massaging his temples gently. "Montana, it wasn't like that!"

"Yes, it was! I read the entire file—every note you wrote about the case. You told me over and over that it was all random. That I had been randomly chosen to carry the bomb into that hotel because I was convenient. You said I'd just been in the wrong place at the wrong time. But that was a lie, wasn't it? You and the whole agency knew I'd been targeted ever since that maid in New York attacked me. I remember exactly what she said. She asked, 'Who are you?' Then when I didn't know what she wanted, she asked me what I knew about the bomb. Now I realize that she somehow knew that I was connected to the leader of the terrorist ring, and she wanted to know who he was."

"You're right. She was hoping to get some information she could use as leverage to get her husband released," Dawson acknowledged, still massaging his temples and closing his eyes as if wishing this was all a bad dream. "In questioning her, we found out that she knew you had been targeted specifically, but she didn't know why. That's what she was trying to figure out. She didn't know how you were involved, but she thought you might know or be connected in some way to the terrorist leader."

"So you lied to me! You brushed it off, making me believe she was just upset at her husband's arrest and lashing out for any way to help him."

"We didn't set out to lie to you. I believe Kelsey told you we thought she was trying to get information out of you, but we didn't tell you all we knew. It was Andrews' orders. He didn't want to alarm you about your own safety, and he thought our investigation into your life would have a better chance of succeeding if you were to behave naturally. If you suddenly started asking questions and investigating your own friends and family, the real person involved in the terrorist ring would disappear, and we would never figure out his connection to you."

"So Andrews assigned you to insert yourself in my life as my boyfriend so you could investigate my friends and family without them or me knowing."

Dawson suddenly stood, came around the desk, and looked her directly in the eye. "Yes," he answered, his blue eyes achingly honest. "That was my assignment on paper. But that wasn't the reality. I love you, Montana."

"You love me? And you expect me to believe that? Is the investigation not over? Do you still have orders to seduce me and maintain our relationship? You used me Dawson! I saw the notes! I know how you expertly manipulated our conversations to find out details about my friends and family. You thoroughly investigated everyone from my father, to my third cousin, to my best friend from second grade and my hair stylist!"

"I had to, Rachel! Yes, it was my assignment, but it was also your life that was at stake! Someone had tried to send you into a hotel with a bomb, fully intending to explode it and kill you in the process!"

"You could have told me what you were doing. You should have told me."

"No, I couldn't. If you had known, you would have blown my cover with your friends and family. Then you would have insisted on helping. From the notes, you should know that the investigation hit a dead end soon after it began. I found no leads. Everyone in your life, including Phillip, checked out. I had nothing to go on. I haven't even been able to work on investigating the Montana side of things for months. I know that's little consolation, but the entire investigation was dead in the water by two months in. Our entire relationship has been real. I haven't even been investigating you since then."

"I know how it works, Dawson. Even if you weren't actively investigating, you were maintaining the position and relationship, watching for any developments. If it was really true that the case was over, you could have come clean about it and told me."

"I wanted to tell you so many times! It was pure torture for me! Montana, I never wanted to hurt you. I was only trying to do my job and protect you at the same time."

"So that's it then? The fact that it was done in the name of protecting me and the country makes it okay? I'm just supposed to accept that the last year of my life has been one huge sham? How can I be okay with the fact that the man I thought I..." Rachel swallowed. She didn't love Dawson. The man she had loved wasn't real. He was just a character Dawson had played to lure her in and entangle himself in her life.

Pushing back all emotion other than anger, she continued. "You deceived me. And this isn't the first time, is it, Dawson? It seems like we've had this conversation before. After everything that happened in Florida with your supposedly fake fiancé, Vanessa Riley, you promised that you would never lie to me again. Do you know how difficult it was for me to trust you after that?"

"I know, Montana. I'm so sorry. I especially wanted to tell you after Florida, but Andrews specifically forbade me from doing so. He was adamant that the Montana angle was still unresolved, and I couldn't inform you until everything was wrapped up. But now it is. We have all the missing pieces, and the case will soon be closed."

"A year ago, you got your assignment from Andrews as I was leaving New York for Helena, right?" Rachel remembered him leaving to talk to Andrews right before she got on the plane.

Dawson nodded.

"Would you have followed me to Helena that day if Andrews hadn't assigned me to you? Would you have met me at the airport and... " Rachel remembered the romance of the moment with his kisses and words. "Would you have been determined to start a relationship with me?"

Dawson looked away, not able to meet her eyes. And she knew: he had only followed her and swept her off her feet because he had been assigned to start a relationship with her.

He finally looked at her. "I wanted you to be mine. I wanted us to be together. But you remember how I had those stupid rules? I honestly don't know if I would have had the courage to follow you and do what my heart really wanted if it hadn't been required."

Dawson reached his hand out to gently touch her face, but she pulled away. "Please, Rachel. Our relationship may not have started with what appears to be honest circumstances, but I cannot be sorry that this assignment gave me the push to pursue and love you the way I wanted to do since the minute I saw you. Now we can put the deception behind us. We can have a clean slate with nothing else hanging over us. What I feel for you has never been a lie. Our relationship, including every word I've said about you and us, even that first time at the Helena airport, has been the absolute truth. I love you. Just give me another chance to show you."

Rachel closed her eyes and swallowed. She remembered all the words of love Dawson had spoken over the past year—everything from his romantic interception at the airport a year ago to their conversation on her parents' porch just a few days ago. They were words that had thrilled her, making her heart pound with their pure love and romance. But now, the memory of those same sweet words held an edge of mockery to them. Lies, every one of them. It had all been an act. He would have never even come to her if he hadn't been required. She had been such a fool.

"No," she said softly. "No more chances. I don't believe a word you say. I told you in Florida that our relationship would be over if I ever found out that you had deceived me again. But I guess that doesn't even apply now, does it? It's not like a relationship that never even existed can be over."

"Rachel, please."

Rachel refused to look at him, refused to acknowledge the pain she could hear in his voice. She knew it was all an act. He was probably just trying to soften the blow by trying to make her think he really did have feelings for her.

"I have a flight to catch," Rachel said, glancing at her watch and moving to the door. With her hand on the doorknob, she stopped. "This is goodbye, Dawson. You're a good agent. You can be satisfied that you did your job well. But it's done now. Don't try to find me. Don't try to contact me. I'll be fine. Just get your things out of my family's guest house and leave me and my life alone. I never want to see or hear from you ever again."

With that, Rachel Saunders exited the room and shut the door on Dawson Tate.

Chapter 25

"Rachel!" Andrews greeted. "I'm glad you made it back to New York! How are you…"

"This is my letter of resignation," Rachel interrupted, sliding the sheet of paper across the desk. "Though I honestly don't know if it's necessary. Do I really need to quit a job that was all part of an elaborate con?"

After boarding the plane in Helena, Rachel had been in so much pain, she had taken one of the stronger pain pills. The flight attendant had woken her when she had to change planes, and then she had slept again until reaching New York mid afternoon. But the drugged sleep hadn't exactly been restful, and Rachel had arrived across the country just as tired, angry, and upset as when she'd left Dawson. She had taken a taxi from the airport to the Homeland Security offices. Using her own computer there, she had written a quick resignation letter and marched into Andrews' office. She just wanted to get this over and go where she could get some real sleep. She could already feel the pain in her shoulder intensifying, but she really wanted to avoid having to take another knock-out pill.

At her words, Andrews' eyes suddenly became very cautious. In silence, he looked her over, probably taking in her disheveled appearance along with the tension and pain she knew were evident on her face. Sighing, he asked gently, "What exactly do you know, Rachel. Or maybe I should say, what do you think you know?"

"I know everything. I know you assigned Dawson Tate to investigate me and my life in Montana. I found Dawson's case file and notes. For the past year, everything about my life has been an elaborate deception in an effort to identify my connection to the origin of the bomb and the terrorist leader."

Andrews shook his head with what seemed to be exasperation. "Rachel, sit down in the chair before you fall over."

Rachel complied, her legs feeling so weak she didn't know how long she could continue standing anyway.

"Now listen. Unfortunately, you don't know everything. If you did, we wouldn't even need to be having this discussion. There are at least two major things you don't know yet. First of all, your position here with Homeland Security was and is not related in any way to Dawson Tate's investigation of the terrorist ring's Montana angle. That was separate entirely. You got and succeeded in your job here based entirely on your own merit and abilities."

"Even if that is true, I still want to quit. How can I continue to work for an agency that deliberately deceived me? Not to mention, there's no way I'd continue working with Dawson as a partner."

Standing up, Andrews turned, opened a large file cabinet, and rummaged through it. Quickly finding what he was looking for, he closed the file drawer and handed the papers to Rachel.

"Remember when you joined Homeland Security?" he asked. "You signed a contract. This is that contract that you signed. Feel free to look it over to refresh your memory."

With a sinking feeling, Rachel remembered signing the contract. She also remembered certain stipulations Andrews had outlined and she had willingly agreed to.

"A year," Rachel said. "The contract was for a year. I remember you saying that you wanted a guarantee that I wasn't just going to join to find Dawson. You thought a year's time would give the agency the chance to evaluate if I was a good investment and give me the chance to decide if this was what I really wanted."

"Exactly."

"But I already know. This is not what I want. I will willingly fulfill my contract. I have about another six months, right? Since you want to hold me to it, maybe you could give me a desk job or something until then. But I'm leaving the minute this contract expires."

"I'm sorry, Rachel, but I don't think that will be possible either."

At her look of confusion, Andrew instructed, "Turn to the fine print on page four."

Rachel scanned the formal, legal terms while Andrews explained, "If you remember, your contract was for a year, but it also had what we call an 'option.' What that means is that Homeland Security was requiring a year to evaluate your performance, and as you said, determine if you were a good investment. After that year, they would have the option to renew your contract."

"Yes, but you also said a year would give me a chance to evaluate if this is what I wanted."

"I believe my words were something to the effect that a year would give you the chance to be more comfortable with a more permanent decision."

Rachel nodded, "Exactly."

"But, unfortunately, Rachel, the contract only grants the 'option' to Homeland Security, not to you."

"What do you mean?" Rachel asked, wary and feeling like she was teetering on the brink of a very high, deadly cliff.

"The Department of Homeland Security does not need your consent to renew your contract at the end of a year. In essence, it is a five year contract with a one year option, kind of like a probation period. If DHS so chooses, you will be under contract for five years. Then and only then will you have the option to resign."

Rachel frantically read and reread the words on the page in front of her. She didn't remember any of this about being locked in for five years. But, with an awful feeling, she did remember that she had been so anxious to find Dawson, she hadn't read the whole contract. Why had she been so stupid? Kelsey had warned her to read every letter of the contract. While Andrews was a good boss, Kelsey had told her that he had ways of getting what he wanted and that he would hold her to every detail of a contract.

She wanted to feel anger at Andrews. He may not have lied to her that day in Florida, but he had definitely led her to believe she was signing a one year, not a five year, contract and that she would be able to quit at the end of a year. Unfortunately, she felt only anger and disgust at herself. She was an adult. She should have read the contract. She'd been warned. Kelsey had even kicked her under the table to remind her not to sign before reading, but she had disregarded her advice and signed the contract anyway.

Andrews was right. DHS could hold her to this contract for five years, and she had no choice. It was all there in black and white, the meaning intermingled through confusing legal phrases and sealed with her very own signature.

"Rachel, I also need to inform you that, even though it's still six months away, DHS will be extending your contract for the full five years. It's not just my decision. My superiors have also taken notice of your performance. Let's just say, DHS has decided you are a very good investment."

Locking eyes with her, Andrews slowly and deliberately slid her letter of resignation back across the desk. "Your request is denied. Your resignation is not accepted."

Rachel closed her eyes, desperation settling in. "I just don't remember going over this in Florida."

"I know we discussed the option, but you may have misunderstood. That part is confusing to most people. But it is right there in the contract. I probably recorded that whole conversation. You know I usually do that with important ones like that. My memory isn't what it used to be. If you want, I can check with my assistant to see if we either have a recording or transcript from that day."

"No," Rachel said, realizing that would be a pointless waste of time. She seriously doubted there was anything wrong with Andrews' memory. Even though she knew he had been less than forthright, she had no one to blame but herself. "I guess it doesn't really matter. I can see that the option is clearly outlined in the contract. I guess I'll have to be a DHS employee for another four and a half years."

"Now, Rachel, don't look so hopeless. You are a great agent, probably the very best I have. Just because we're holding you to a five year contract doesn't mean we won't be willing to work with you. It's not like we want someone working as an agent when they really don't want to be. Your job is too dangerous for that. It would put the agent, the investigation, and everyone else at risk to not have someone fully committed to the job.

"So I want you to give it some thought, Rachel. What is it you would like to do here? If you name it, I will find a way to make it happen. I don't think you'd truly be happy working at a desk. Like I said, you're the best I've got, so I'd like to see you stay an agent. However, we might be able to have you do some training of other agents or maybe even work more as a contractor of sorts. You could get your choice of cases and only work the ones you want. You don't have to work with Tate. We could assign you a different partner, or you could just work independently."

"Thank you, sir. I appreciate that. I'll give it some thought and get back to you." Rachel knew Andrews didn't have to work with her in any way, let alone offer to let her name her position and job description.

Rachel stood to leave, suddenly feeling claustrophobic. All of the events from the past year felt as if they were closing in on her. She had no control over what had happened, and now she would really have no control over her life for another four and a half years. She knew she needed to get out of that office before she completely lost it.

"Rachel," Andrews called.

Rachel turned from the door.

"I know you've been through a lot." For the first time today, Rachel saw care and sympathy in her boss's face. "I know it's no consolation, but you did an excellent job on this case. You were the one to figure out Phillip was our guy. We didn't have a clue. When your dad couldn't find you, Kelsey checked the security footage and found where you went. By your body language, they knew you had figured something out. Honestly, I wasn't convinced, but I gave Tate and Matthews permission to go check it out with your dad. I was too busy taking care of the mess we had upstairs. Everyone on this case has done a good job, but you are the sole reason we have it solved. There's no telling how many lives you saved."

Rachel nodded, appreciating what Andrews was not saying. He was not mentioning that those lives would have been taken by her own brother. He was not saying that Phillip Saunders was now in custody and probably facing life in prison.

Andrews continued gently, "Take as much time off as you need to get your head back on straight. Then we'll talk about what you want to do."

Rachel nodded and wordlessly turned back around.

"And Rachel," Andrews said, interrupting her departure once again. "You might want to give Tate a chance to explain. I somehow doubt you have the full story yet."

Rachel walked out of the office. She somehow made it out of the building and into a taxi. On impulse, she gave the driver the name of a hotel. She should just go home to the apartment she shared with Kelsey, but she couldn't make herself do it. She wanted to run away and hide. She wanted to go somewhere no one could find her.

As the taxi drove through the streets of New York, the full reality of what had happed with both Phillip and Dawson began to sink in. The numbness and anger faded, and she began to feel heart-wrenching agony.

Rachel tried to focus on the weather. She just needed something mundane to distract her. She closed her eyes and took deep breaths. It was pretty hot and muggy today here in New York.

Just keep breathing. In… and out.

Keep it together, Rachel. Just make it to the hotel. You can fall apart there. Just make it to the hotel!

Chapter 26

Rachel didn't know how she checked into the hotel and made it to her room. The instant she shut the door, she fell apart. She collapsed back against the door and slid down. Great wracking sobs gripped her body. She couldn't breathe.

Every aspect of her life had been a lie. Her brother. Her boyfriend. Andrews had said she had done a good job, but she should have figured it out sooner. How naive and gullible she was! How could she have not known her brother was a terrorist?

Rachel curled into a fetal position on the carpet and sobbed, her heart feeling like it was literally breaking in half. Memories of Phillip danced through her head. Suddenly every little look, every little phrase he'd ever said that didn't make sense, had a new meaning. Not only had Phillip robbed her family's future, he'd robbed their past. How could they ever remember their lives with

Phillip and not feel the pain and bitterness of his deception and betrayal?

As soon as this story hit the media, her family would be under the spotlight of an entire country. There would be no sympathy, only ridicule. Every little aspect of Phillip's life and their own family would be uncovered for public scrutiny. What kind of parents could raise a son intent on attacking and murdering his own countrymen? What kind of sister wouldn't know that her older brother was an evil mastermind? In that moment, Rachel felt that she could not survive what she knew was coming, let alone help her parents through the coming nightmare.

And then when her relentless brain had filed through every memory and agony with Phillip, memories of the last year with Dawson began their taunting dance. The scene from the beach in Florida almost six months ago replayed through her mind, Dawson's longed-for words now mocking her.

"I can't stop loving you. Please don't ask me to. You're the only woman I've ever loved. The only one I will ever love. Do you understand, Montana? I love you, I love you, ... I love you."

It had been the first time Dawson had told her he loved her. But now she knew it had all been a performance. He had been required to entice her into a relationship so he could investigate her. Then when it looked as if she might end it, he had to do something to maintain their relationship and his position in her life. He had told her exactly what she had wanted to hear. Only now, those same words were needles, unmercifully pricking her already broken heart.

She had loved him! Passionately. Completely. Now it was over. He didn't love her. He had never loved her.

Rachel gasped, unable to get control. She had never been the type to have meltdowns. It usually took an extraordinary amount of stress and trauma for her to completely lose it. On those few occasions where she had been overwhelmed, someone had always been there to comfort and help her through. She remembered her mom or dad holding her when she had finally reached her limit as a child. After everything that had happened a year ago in New York, Dawson had been there to hold her as she released all the pent-up tension and emotion. Then again, after she had to pull the trigger and kill a man in Florida, Dawson had been there to whisper words of encouragement and comfort.

Now there was no one.

Her entire world had fallen apart. Her family was forever and irreversibly broken. The man she loved had deceived her and was now gone from her life. She had reached the end of herself and there was no one left to pick up the pieces.

Rachel tried to move away from the door, crawling toward the bed. Eyes blurred, she struggled up onto the mattress and curled into a ball. Complete agony overwhelmed her and she lost track of time as she cried out her grief.

"God, help me!" she moaned, begging for relief and mercy. "Please, please, help me!"

Rachel had been a Christian for a long time, but she tended to take her faith for granted. Though Rachel trusted God for her salvation and was fully committed to having him be the boss of her life, she hadn't ever felt the real need to have him be involved in her everyday existence. Sure, she had turned to God to help her get out of the dangerous situations she had encountered in the past year, but for the most part, she was independent and very self-sufficient. She honestly hadn't had to depend on God that much because she had always been able to use her own strength and abilities to manage the difficulties in her life. But now, she had no one to help her manage the trauma and pain, and she nothing left in and of herself to handle this.

And so… she surrendered to the only One who could handle it.

Rachel found herself praying that God would take the broken mess she was and do with it as He willed. She knew she had nothing left to give, but all she had, all she was, she offered to Him. She had no idea what to do with her life—no clue how to even make it through the next few minutes.

In the midst of her prayer, she felt a subtle peace wash over her, along with the comfort of knowing that she wasn't really alone. The intense pain was still there, but so was an assurance that He would see her through. It felt almost as if huge, loving arms wrapped themselves around her, lifting her, and taking her to a place that no longer seemed so dark.

Then her prayers changed. Instead of surrendering and seeking mercy, she began to be thankful, praising God for his comfort and love. She wasn't aware of when her conversation with God melted into blessed sleep.

She didn't even realize she had fallen asleep until she gradually became aware of someone pounding on the door. Rachel was disoriented as she surfaced from her cocoon of sleep to wakefulness. Gradually, she remembered what had happened and where she was.

And still, the relentless pounding on the door continued.

"Rachel, open up! I know you're in there."

Rachel recognized the voice.

Groggy, she stumbled out of bed and headed for the door. What time was it anyway? She glanced at her watch. 9:00 AM. Had she really slept all night?

"Rachel, if you don't open up, I'll use my DHS badge and get management to let me in! Open this door and let me in right now!"

Rachel turned the knob and opened the door wide.

Garrett.

Chapter 27

"You sound like the Big, Bad Wolf," Rachel grumbled as Garrett entered the room.

"And you look like I'm too late. You must have been attacked by another wolf before I got here."

Rachel ran a hand through her tangled hair, knowing she must look absolutely terrible.

"What do you want, Garrett. I'm not really in the mood for a social call."

"I came to check on you. I saw Andrews. He was worried about you, and of course, Dawson is beside himself."

"How did you find me?" Rachel asked. She had specifically come to a hotel because she hadn't wanted to be found.

"Come on, Rachel. You're a DHS agent. This time, at least, you managed to have both your cell phone and your watch with you."

Of course. Rachel really needed to do a better job of remembering her government-issued locaters when she wanted to be found and forgetting them when she didn't.

Garrett's eyes raked over her, seeming to assess her emotional state along with every other detail in her appearance. "You're having a pretty rough time, aren't you, Rachel." It wasn't a question. It was a diagnosis.

Rachel sighed and sat on the bed, criss-crossing her legs like she had in kindergarten.

"You already missed my complete meltdown, Garret. I'm actually doing better right now. I know my parents and I are not going to have an easy road ahead of us. It's going to be hard enough dealing with the knowledge of who Phillip is, but when this hits the media…"

Garrett sat on the bed beside her. "I don't think that's going to be a problem, Rachel. There was no attack. DHS makes arrests and thwarts terrorist plots all the time, and the public is never the wiser. The only reason the Riley case was different was because he was so well known. Phillip Saunders, though wealthy and influential in the business world, is more of the up-and-coming sort. He doesn't have the same long-standing reputation John Riley had. Remember the whole incident in New York a year ago wasn't even mentioned in the media. I know for a fact that DHS is not planning on releasing any information on this case to the public. Sometimes the less the American people know, the better. And this would probably fall into that category. All they need to know is that DHS is actively working and succeeding at keeping them safe."

"But what about all those people at the Governor's Ball? They saw the Lieutenant Governor of Montana get arrested. I somehow doubt the Lieutenant Governor is going to be okay with having everything brushed under the table. He'll want to have his name cleared."

"Oh, he'll have his name cleared, but we'll do it with minimum details. You'd probably be surprised, but he was actually very cooperative. I think he was just relieved. He was very understanding when we explained the situation and how he had been used as a decoy. He really had no knowledge of what was happening. The other hotel employee was definitely with the terrorists, but he was just following orders to frame the Lieutenant Governor and create a good distraction so Phillip and Vanessa could get away. He did pass a small memory card to the Lieutenant Governor, but it was completely blank. The Lieutenant Governor is somewhat computer illiterate and didn't even know what the thing was."

"So he's okay with the full details not being released to the papers?"

"Oh, yes. Just enough information will be given to clear his name and even make him look a little heroic in the public eye. This isn't the first terrorist plot that DHS has stopped in the past few years. In fact, terrorist cells seem to be specifically targeting the Northwest as the ideal place to base their operations. As in this case, the isolated, rustic setting makes it easier to go unnoticed."

"What about Phillip? He was transferred to a secure location, but do you know what's going on?"

"He's being questioned. I know he'll face charges for a variety of crimes, including treason and Amir's murder. The case against him is pretty airtight. Vanessa Riley is already singing like a bird, trying to cut a deal for a lesser sentence. Hopefully, Phillip will talk as well and take a plea bargain instead of going to trial and facing the death penalty."

Rachel shivered involuntarily at the mere thought of her brother facing such a fate.

Garrett paused and reached out, taking Rachel's hand in his. "I'm so sorry, Rachel. None of us even suspected Phillip. Sure, we thought he was an annoying jerk, but we thought he was harmless.

After everything you've been through and everything he did, I can't imagine what you're feeling."

"Did you know?" Rachel asked abruptly. "You said 'none of us even suspected Phillip.' But did you know I was assigned to Dawson as an asset and that he was investigating my friends and family in connection with the New York attempted bombing?"

"No, Rachel," Garrett, replied, his honest eyes meeting her own. "I didn't know. I suspected something like that though. Even back in Florida, I knew Dawson had some other secret he was keeping from you. I just didn't know what it was. I could tell it was bothering him and eating him up inside, but no, I didn't know until he told me himself after you left Helena."

"You warned me back in Florida," Rachel said softly. "You told me he would break my heart. I didn't listen."

Garrett was quiet, his hand still gently holding hers. He looked at her, his eyes dark and hooded, and somehow, Rachel knew what he was thinking. He was recalling that evening on the beach in Miami. He was remembering the passion of their kiss. She saw his gaze focus on her lips, and she knew he wanted to kiss her once again.

But she didn't want him to.

Back in Miami, she had been so angry and confused, not knowing how she felt about Dawson or if she even wanted to try to salvage a relationship with him. Now she knew there was no hope for their relationship, but she also knew she was irreversibly in love with him. Even if the Dawson Tate she loved was just a facade who didn't really exist, she didn't know that she could ever love another man the same way.

"Rachel, I'm going to be honest with you," Garrett said, looking away from her face and studying their clasped hands. Rachel watched his handsome face as he seemed to struggle to find the right words.

Finally, Garrett spoke, his quiet voice heavy with tightly-controlled emotion. "I would like nothing better than to take you in my arms, kiss you senseless, and make you forget all about Dawson Tate. But I can't."

Garrett paused, shutting his eyes briefly before continuing resolutely. "While my feelings for you haven't changed in the past six months… Dawson has become my friend. He's helped me with a lot of things I had been struggling with, including my relationship with God. I've watched him. I've tried to find some kind of hypocrisy in him, but I've found none. That isn't to say that we don't have our differences. He's arrogant and grates on my nerves. I'll still probably disagree with him on just about everything, especially if it relates to work or you. But I respect him. Despite what you may think, he is genuine, and he loves you."

"How can you say that?" Rachel said, exasperated. She tried to remove her hand from Garrett's, but he held it firmly. "I was his assignment!"

"I don't know the details," Garrett admitted. "For him, I think his feelings for you and the case were two entirely separate things. We talk and text on the phone pretty regularly. I could tell something has been bothering him for months, but he wouldn't tell me what it was. I think it tortured him to deceive you. Even back in Florida, I would catch him looking at you with a frightened, almost sick expression on his face. I think he wanted to tell you, but the thought of losing you scared him to death."

Though Rachel was relieved that Garrett wouldn't be trying to step in and pressure her into a relationship, it surprised her that he and Dawson had developed such a good friendship since Miami. Usually it seemed like they didn't like each other at all. She knew that Dawson had mentioned talking to Garrett, but she had always assumed it was work related."

Rachel shook her head. "Dawson always seems genuine, but this is the second time in a year that he's masterminded an elaborate deception while appearing to be genuine the entire time. I don't know where the truth is with him. Maybe he doesn't know himself. There's nothing left for us. Our entire relationship was based on him deceiving me so he could investigate my life. He admitted that he wouldn't have initially followed me and begun our relationship if he hadn't been forced to do so."

"Rachel, it doesn't matter how the relationship began. The fact is that he loves you. I think deep down, you know he loves you. You know he's genuine. He was just doing his job, and in this case, his personal and professional life collided. You're understandably hurt and angry, but I think you're trying to throw up even more reasons to distance yourself from him."

Rachel was quiet. Was there even a possibility that Garrett was right? Had Dawson been just as much of a victim of circumstances as she was? Had he really been honest about the person he was and what he'd said to her? Did he truly love her?

"Look, Rachel. I know that, at this point, you and I have no shot at a relationship. Whether or not you want to admit it, you love Dawson. And it's not the kind of love that goes away because you're hurt and mad. So you have a choice. You're going to have to decide if you want to hang on to some very justified anger and bitterness and lose Dawson Tate, or if you want to let go of that and give the man you love another chance. Don't get me wrong, you are fully entitled to be very angry at being so deceived. Looking just at the facts, you should ditch the guy for yours truly and never speak his name again. That would be the right thing to do. But, as much as it pains me, I think you're going to have to decide if you want to be right or if you want to be happy."

Finally, having extracted her hand from Garrett's, Rachel rubbed her temples, suddenly very tired. She had slept all night, but now her shoulder was hurting and she just didn't feel like she could emotionally handle thinking about this anymore.

"Thank you, Garrett," she said. "I appreciate your input. I'll give it some thought, but right now I really need to eat something, take some meds, and get cleaned up."

"You probably need some more rest as well," Garrett said, standing. "I have to get back to work anyway. I checked in at the office right after my flight from Helena landed, but since Andrews and I were both concerned, I had to check on you first."

"Thanks, Garrett, I appreciate it."

"Oh, and Andrews said to tell you to check your email. He sent you something you need to see ASAP."

"Okay," she said.

As Garrett reached the door, Rachel impulsively wrapped her arms around him in a brief hug. "You're a good friend, Garrett. Thanks for everything."

As she released him, she saw a strange look on his face. He reached out and gently pushed back a strand of hair from her cheek. His eyes were filled with longing, maybe even love. Garrett blinked and dropped his hand, but in that one instant, Rachel realized how difficult this was for him to not try to fill Dawson's void in her life. She only had a vague idea of how much he really cared, but she respected him all the more for his restraint and integrity.

"Rachel, if..." he began, the longing seeping into his voice. But then he shook his head, never finishing the thought. Smiling at her sadly, he turned and walked out.

Rachel took a deep, shuddering breath and found that her entire body was shaking. Finding a menu by the phone, she quickly ordered some room service. She didn't remember the last time she'd eaten. She thought she'd eaten something at some point yesterday, but she didn't remember where or when.

Rachel walked restlessly around the room. They had said her food wouldn't take long to deliver, but even fifteen minutes was too long. She didn't want to think about Phillip or Dawson. She was feeling better now and didn't want to dissolve into tears again.

Desperate for distraction, she picked up her phone. She saw Dawson's nineteen missed calls, but there was no way she was going to call him back.

She flipped over to her email. She really had no desire to even open the message from Andrews, but for lack of something else to do, she opened it anyway.

The message was only one line: "Listen to this."

Attached to the email was an audio file. Accustomed to her boss's sometimes cryptic orders, Rachel opened the file.

Her heart leapt painfully. It was Dawson's voice.

Chapter 28

"You wanted to see me?" Dawson asked.

"Yes, I have a new assignment for you." With the sound of Andrews' voice, Rachel immediately realized she was listening to one of his recordings. He had told her before that he made a habit of recording important conversations with his agents, such as when he gave assignments. While he claimed this was to assist his failing memory, Rachel knew it was probably more for liability reasons and to keep the agents accountable.

"Okay," Dawson responded, his voice sounding wary.

"Rachel Saunders. Your assignment is Rachel Saunders."

With the mention of her own name, Rachel realized she was listening to a recording from almost a year ago, when Andrews had assigned Dawson to investigate her.

She felt ill and collapsed back on the bed. Why would Andrews want her to hear this? It would be like kicking someone who was already down. But no matter how sick she may feel, she couldn't bring herself to stop the recording from revealing every last agonizing detail.

"What exactly do you mean?" Dawson asked, the caution in his voice now only more evident.

Andrews replied, "Your assignment is to insert yourself into Rachel Saunders' life. I'll leave the nature of the relationship up to you, of course. From what we learned from the maid who attacked her at the hotel, we strongly suspect that Saunders was specifically chosen to be the mule for that bomb. The maid was apparently persuaded that Saunders knew the leader of the terrorist ring, and she was trying to get that information. We have to act on that same assumption."

"Sir, I would much prefer to inform Rachel Saunders of the situation, including the fact that her life may still be at risk. The person who wanted her dead may not give up. Plus, she's smart. She may be able to help us figure out who's after her."

"Protecting her will, of course, be part of your job. But no. Saunders is to know nothing of what we learned from the maid or your true reason for being in her life. She is currently under the impression that all of these events were random. We need to keep her under that illusion. It's obvious that she has no clue who may be involved in a terrorist ring and no clue who may want her dead. She needs to behave as naturally as possible while you investigate absolutely everyone in her life. If she knows anything of this investigation, she may behave unnaturally and tip off this person we're looking for. The minute he suspects anything, he will disappear, and the lead will dry up."

"Sir," Dawson said, his voice tense. "I've never refused an assignment. But I'm really not comfortable deceiving Rachel Saunders in this way."

"Why not? You've deceived other women many times before in both short and long-term investigations. This time is no different. May I remind you what is at stake? We have not apprehended everyone involved in this. This terrorist ring is not likely to stop with an unsuccessful attempt. If we don't follow this lead to find everyone involved, we may enable them to plot and follow through with a massively destructive attack."

"I know I've worked undercover on other cases, but this time is different," Dawson said quietly. "I cannot deceive her. I won't. Sir, I care about her too much. Where Rachel Saunders is concerned, I'm too personally involved to do what you ask as an undercover agent in her life."

"But that's exactly why you're the perfect agent for the job! You already have an existing connection with her, and she trusts you. Whereas most undercover investigations take a lot of time for the agent to even maneuver into the right position, you'll already be there in the perfect place to investigate her life. This is what we need."

"No, Sir," Dawson said flatly. Rachel recognized only too well the steely determination lacing his voice. "I'm sorry. I simply can't do what you ask. I can't deceive her that way. Give me a different assignment. There has to be a different angle of this case I can work. But, as far as the assignment to be an undercover agent in Rachel Saunders' life, I refuse."

There was silence. Though Rachel knew this was a conversation that had happened almost a year ago, she could still feel the tension of the moment, like a rubber band was stretched taut between the two men.

After almost thirty seconds of what Rachel imagined must have been an intense staring contest, Andrews spoke. "I don't recall that assignments have ever been optional for my agents, unless you have a stipulation in your contract that I don't know about,

Tate. That being said, you are aware that I don't want agents on cases they aren't fully committed to. It's too dangerous, and I won't get the results I need. If you feel that strongly against investigating Rachel Saunders, then we'll find a different assignment for you."

"Thank you, Sir," Dawson replied, the relief in his tone evident.

Andrews continued, "There is another angle to this case that we will be working, but we're still a few weeks out from having enough intel for you to go forward with an investigation. I'm beginning to think this attempted bombing goes a lot deeper than we originally thought. We need to finish interrogating the terrorist suspects we have apprehended, but the curious thing is that I'm sure a large percentage of them are Americans. We suspect there's someone from Saunders' life involved, but I doubt he or she is the only one. I think we're going to have to compile a suspect list of wealthy Americans who might have the power and position to fund something like this."

"If you get me the list, I'll take it from there and see what I can find out."

"Will do. But just so you know, I can't abandon the investigation of Saunders and the Montana angle of this case. It's too important. Since you are unwilling to do it, I will assign it to Garrett Matthews. He's not in your unique position of already being acquainted with Saunders, but he's an excellent agent. He seems her type, or at least he will be very good at pretending to be. I'm sure she would like him a great deal, and it won't take him long to position himself in her life."

"No." Dawson's voice was almost a growl. "Not Garrett Matthews."

"You're not leaving me much of a choice here, Dawson. You don't want the case, and yet I have to have that intel. So…"

"I'll do it!" Dawson interrupted.

"I don't understand," Andrews's tone was confused, but Rachel also knew him well enough to recognize when he was manipulating a situation and thoroughly enjoying it. "You said you wanted nothing to do with this case. I don't want an agent who doesn't want…"

"I do want it!" Dawson practically yelled. Then he continued more calmly. "Nobody but me goes near Rachel, understand? If you're going to insist on Rachel being investigated, I'll get you the intel. Just leave her alone."

"If you're sure…"

"I'm sure. You win, Andrews. Get me on a plane for Montana ASAP. This is my case now. Anything involving Rachel Saunders is mine."

Chapter 29

Dusk was just beginning to fall as Rachel got into the waiting taxi and gave the driver the name of her hotel. She didn't know why she'd even bothered. Shopping was stressful, not therapeutic! Sure, she had found the dress she'd wanted, but that would do her absolutely no good since she'd been unable to get tickets to the Broadway show she'd intended to wear it to. They claimed they were sold out for the next two months!

Rachel sighed and looked at the list in the small notebook she carried in her purse. Maybe she could wear the dress to something else.

After moping around her hotel for a few hours and unsuccessfully trying to sleep, Rachel had developed a plan. She had always wanted to see the sights of New York. That hadn't happened with that initial ill-fated trip that she had 'won' a year ago. Even though she had been living here in New York off and on for almost six months now, she still hadn't gotten to see much. Both she and Dawson had been so busy with work when in New York that they hadn't gotten to do much. She had been able to talk Kelsey into taking those dance lessons when Dawson was gone on another assignment, but that had been it. Kelsey wasn't really interested in seeing the sights. She had grown up in New York, and besides that, she wasn't much of a tourist anyway.

Figuring distraction was the best way to deal with the overwhelming stress in her life, Rachel made a list of things she wanted to do or see. She had enough money to spend a couple more days in the hotel, and she intended to fully pretend she was on vacation. After that, she would go back to her own apartment, talk to Andrews, make decisions she didn't want to deal with, and get back to the problems of the real world. Somewhere in there she would request to go back to Montana to see her parents. She knew she wouldn't be able to work in any capacity without seeing first-hand that they were okay.

At least not everything was going badly, Rachel thought, trying to comfort herself. She had talked to both her mom and dad earlier this afternoon, and they were both handling Phillip's betrayal and arrest better than she had expected. Yes, they were devastated and feeling every emotion from anger to guilt and shame, but somehow Rachel was confident they would be able to get through this. Her parents had a strong faith, and she knew that they were praying, not that Phillip would be released, but that God would use whatever was necessary to get his attention in such a way that would save his soul and radically change his life.

Rachel had also called and talked to Kelsey for quite a while. As usual, Kelsey was a good listener, not saying a lot, but offering words of comfort and reassurance when necessary. Like Garrett, Kelsey was confident that the story, even the aspect involving the Lieutenant Governor, had already been handled and would not be leaked to the media. She had listened to Rachel's turmoil about Dawson and the recording she had heard, but she hadn't tried to offer advice other than to say that Rachel should pray about it. That in itself was a little strange considering Kelsey had never claimed to be a Christian, but she knew Rachel was.

And Rachel had been praying. Even though she was doing her best to distract herself from her problems, it seemed like the pain and stress would try to overwhelm her every few minutes. Feeling helpless at the onslaught, she would pray, depending on God for help and peace to get her through and guide her in the right direction. So far, He had definitely answered on the peace part, but she was still waiting for direction.

Dawson had continued to relentlessly call her cell phone, but she couldn't answer, not yet. She didn't even know what to say if she did answer. If anything, the recording Andrews had sent her had only confused her more. She knew now that Dawson hadn't willingly taken the case of investigating her. He had cared about her from the very beginning and hadn't wanted to deceive her. He had only consented to do it when Andrews had manipulated him and backed him in the corner. Rachel even got some absurd delight from knowing that Dawson had taken the case to prevent Garrett from doing it. He'd cared too much and been too jealous to even think about letting another man in her life other than him!

However, none of that changed the fact that Rachel was extremely hurt and didn't know if she would ever be able to trust Dawson again. He was an accomplished liar. It was part of his job. What if something else happened and he lied to her again? She would never be able to know when he was telling the truth and when he wasn't!

Just looking at the facts on the surface, she knew she should never speak to Dawson again. This was the second time in one year that he had created an elaborate deception involving her. Sure, both instances had been in the name of investigations to protect the American people, but that still didn't change the fact that he'd romanced Vanessa Riley and her at the same time. Then he'd gotten engaged to Vanessa and been planning a wedding, all the while keeping Rachel blissfully clueless to his double life. Then after promising never to lie to her again, Rachel now finds out that their entire relationship had been built on deception. He had only pursued her because he'd been assigned to do so. Yes, he had cared, but he would have never followed her, never loved her, if he hadn't been doing his job.

So what should she do?

She didn't even know for sure what Dawson wanted. Maybe he really wanted to get back to his original life without her in it, but if he didn't... If he really loved her and still wanted a relationship with her, should she refuse? Would she have the courage to give him one more chance, even if her heart wanted her to?

As the taxi weaved its way through the streets of New York, Rachel paid no attention. Though her eyes were on the silly list of things she wanted to do, her mind floated back over her relationship with Dawson. She remembered when she was leaving New York the first time and Dawson drove her to the airport. He hadn't intended to have a relationship with her. He had been trying to explain that, though they shared an amazing connection, he didn't want to even attempt to be involved with her. He'd told her all his rules, basically excuses that would keep them apart. In return, she had taunted him, shooting down every one of his rules by sarcastically agreeing that there were never any exceptions that would allow them to have a successful relationship anyway, so why try?

She clearly remembered taunting, "Wow, Dawson, stick to those rules and you'll never get hurt."

Now her own words tormented her. If she gave up on Dawson, he would never be able to hurt her again. There would be no risk. She would never have to feel the same excruciating ache of being deceived and having her heart broken. She could heal and move on with her life. Maybe Dawson had been right after all.

"Rachel,... you're going to have to decide if you want to be right or if you want to be happy."

Garrett's words from earlier today haunted her. She hadn't been able to escape them. Every time her mind analyzed every last detail and potential consequence of her relationship with Dawson, it always circled back to Garrett's words. Did she want to take the risk-free escape route to do what would be most logical and end it completely with Dawson? Could she ever really be happy without this man she had loved so deeply? Did she want to be right or did she want to be happy?

"Excuse me, Miss," the taxi driver said.

Rachel's head immediately snapped to attention.

"A friend of mine asked that I give this to you," he said, passing her an envelope.

Still feeling a little dazed from being forced back to reality so suddenly, Rachel's hand automatically took the envelope. She started to ask who his friend was, but stopped as her curiosity over the white rectangle took over. With her history and training, she was naturally paranoid of unidentified packages, but this looked harmless enough. It's not like a bomb could fit inside. The only marking was 'Rachel' written across the front, and it wasn't even sealed.

Flipping up the back flap, Rachel removed three pieces of paper from inside. Unfolding the first, she found a map of New York. Different well-known landmarks were circled, along with a few she didn't recognize. Beside one such circle was written, 'IOU dinner'.

Rachel was confused. Nobody owed her dinner. Who could have sent this? What did the map mean? Lifting it up, she looked at the two other, smaller pieces of paper. They were tickets. The very tickets to the Broadway show she had wanted to see. She looked at the date. They were for tomorrow night.

"We're here, Miss," the taxi driver announced.

Rachel had been so focused, she hadn't realized the taxi had stopped. She didn't even know how long the driver had been waiting for her to get out.

"Oh, sorry!" She said, embarrassed and frantically gathering the papers, her purse, and the dress she had purchased. "How much do I owe you?"

Rachel handed him the amount he named, along with a generous tip, and hurriedly crawled out of the cab. Later, she realized that she should have asked him more about the envelope. She should have at least tried to find out who his friend was. But, at that particular moment, she was too disoriented and embarrassed to do more than get out of that taxi as fast as she could.

Standing on the curb, she struggled to get a better grip on things with her injured shoulder held immobile in its sling. Finally straightening, Rachel looked up.

This was not her hotel.

But with a sudden shock, she recognized exactly what hotel it was.

The Intercontinental Times Square.

This is where it had all started. This was where she was to have stayed a year ago on her 'prize' trip to New York. This was where she was to have taken the bomb in her suitcase. This very curb was where her life had changed when she'd been intercepted by…

Dawson came toward her. Was she dreaming? She saw him smile as he closed the distance between them, but his eyes were still… afraid? This couldn't be happening, not again!

Before she could find her voice to ask Dawson what was going on, he had reached her. Without pausing, he wrapped his arms around her and kissed her passionately. At the touch of his lips, Rachel melted. All worry, all coherent thought vanished. She fully returned his kiss, desperately, passionately, not caring beyond the oasis of this single moment. Oh, how she loved him!

Finally breaking the kiss, he continued to hold her close as his shallow breath whispered in her ear. "I love you, Montana. Please don't kill me. I told you once that I planned on taking my life into my own hands and thoroughly kissing you on a regular basis.

But I have to confess, I've never been so nervous about it before."

Rachel stepped back and looked at him. He did look really nervous. He thought she might actually beat him up!

She laughed, "Don't worry, Hollywood, I have no intention of practicing any martial arts on you at the moment."

At the tone of her voice and the use of his nickname, Dawson looked hopeful for the first time.

Suddenly unsure, Rachel looked away. What should she say? What did she want? Yes, she had kissed him, but…

"You're done with the investigation in Montana already?" she asked, latching onto the first question she could think of.

"Yes. We still have some things to wrap up, but I've had some strong motivation to get my part done. I had to see you."

"You owe me dinner?" Rachel asked suddenly, remembering the map from the taxi. Dawson must have been the one to have arranged all of this.

Thankfully, Dawson was able to keep up with her rapid change of subject. "Remember when I first met you here and you didn't know there was a bomb in your suitcase? I told you I was going to take you dinner. Then we got into the taxi, things kind of turned crazy, and I never took you to dinner. I know you had wanted to see New York on that trip, and I got to thinking that, with everything going on the past year, you had never really gotten to do that. If you would let me Montana, I'd like to take you to do all those things now."

Rachel still didn't look at him. She knew he was being sweet. Part of her wanted to jump back into his arms and let him make her forget all of the problems. But she just didn't know.

What exactly was he feeling? What did he want?

Rachel felt Dawson's finger under her chin, urging her to look at him. Reluctantly, she met his eyes, knowing that her pain and uncertainty were probably still there for him to see.

The minute Dawson's eyes met hers, she couldn't look away. For as she was letting him see the depths of her soul, he was letting her see his. She recognized his pain, his fear, his love.

"Rachel, I love you. I am so sorry to have caused you pain. Please forgive me. But I can't be sorry that this investigation gave me the push I needed to pursue you. I was such an idiot to have needed a push to begin with, but the fact is that I am hopelessly, forever in love with you. Please, let me be a part of your life again."

Eyes still locked with Rachel, Dawson slowly, deliberately dropped to one knee. He didn't seem to care that he was kneeling on the hard sidewalk or that he was now attracting the stares and giggles of people passing by. Out of the corner of her eye, Rachel even saw a few people taking pictures with their phones.

With shaking hands, Dawson opened a small box, revealing a breathtaking diamond ring.

"I've had this ring for about four months now. I even asked your dad's permission months ago. At this point, he's probably wondering what's taking me so long. But I couldn't give you this ring before you knew the entire truth. And now that you do, I can't wait another day without letting you know how I truly feel."

Rachel was stunned and having trouble even processing what was happening. In some ways, Dawson's features looked as if he was going on a suicide mission. *He thinks I'm going to flat-out refuse him!*

Yet Rachel also recognized the love and determination consuming the depths of his gaze. He was going to do this no matter what the results.

"Montana, I can't live without you. But I can't ask you to give me one more chance because, honestly, I'll probably need a lot more than that.

With God's help, I want to make you happy and prove to you every day, for the rest of our lives, just how much I love you. I think I've loved you since the first moment I saw you arguing with the attendant at the airport. But that love was nothing compared to how much I loved you after everything we went through here in New York. And that love was nothing compared with how much more I've fallen in love with you over the past year as you rescued and forgave me in Miami and then handled everything that has been thrown your way recently. Now I love you so hopelessly that I can't see straight. I can't promise that I won't ever hurt you again, but I can promise that I will spend every day for the rest of my life loving you and falling more deeply in love with you. Please, Rachel Leigh Saunders—my Montana. Will you marry me?

And with Dawson's question, Rachel decided to be happy.

She knelt on the sidewalk in front of him and offered him her left hand

"Yes, Dawson. Yes."

She watched as a look of utter joy dawned on his face. With firm, yet shaking hands, he put the ring on her finger.

Then she kissed him.

For better or worse, she loved him. She knew what made sense. She knew what the facts demanded she should do. But, for Dawson Tate, she would make an exception.

Please enjoy the following Sneak Peek of

Yesterday

Time Travel Romance / Christian Romantic Suspense

Chapter 1

Red flashed against the bright white of the snow.

I slammed on the brakes. The SUV skidded toward the guardrail.

My heart seemed to stop. I couldn't breathe. My body felt suspended as the mountainous terrain whirled across my vision. I braced for impact. Unexpectedly, the vehicle lurched as the tires found traction and came to a sudden stop

I sucked in air. My eyes frantically searched the heavy snowfall.

What had I seen?

Was it human?

Had I hit something?

The Sierra mountains were shrouded in the stillness of the winter storm, silent and revealing no secrets. Had I just imagined something dart in front of me?

I caught a glimpse of a fist out of the corner of my eye. I jumped. A strangled scream escaped my throat as the fist started hammering on my window. Heart thumping, I peered beyond the relentless pounding to see the outline of a woman in a red parka. She was screaming, but I couldn't understand her words.

Fingers fumbling and shaking, I rolled down my window. At her appearance, an electric current of shock ripped through me.

Blood streamed from somewhere on her head. It trickled down to her chin, leaving a dark red trail. Dirty tears streaked her cheeks, and her hair hung in clumps of frizzy knots.

I frantically jerked open my door.

"Are you okay?" I asked.

But she didn't answer. Instead, she continued to scream, her hysterical cries now slicing through me.

"Help! Help! Please help me! I can't get them out!"

What was she talking about? My eyes traced an invisible line to where she was gesturing. A few yards in front of my own fender, the meager guardrail was bent and scraped. Peering through the falling snow, I could see beyond that to where the frozen earth had been torn up. Standing on the frame of my car door, I looked into the embankment off the side. Red tail lights glowed like beacons.

The shock to my senses was like a physical blow. I sprang out of the car, stepping into a blood stained patch of snow. Blood had dripped from the woman's leg where her torn pants exposed a jagged wound. Her sobbing and frantic cries continued, but she wasn't making sense.

Her skin was chalky green. She was in shock, yet I felt paralyzed. My medical background consisted of a three hour CPR and first aid class I'd taken over a year ago. Panic washed over me like a wave. I didn't know how to help her!

Desperate, I gently pushed her toward the back seat of the SUV. Her feet shuffled forward two steps, and then she collapsed. I caught her around the shoulders and practically dragged her rag doll frame to the back seat.

She roused enough to help as I lifted her into the back seat. I unraveled the scarf from my neck and wrapped it around her leg above the bloody gash, tying it as tightly as I could.

Reaching into the back of the SUV, I located a large flashlight and my old coat that I used when skiing. I wrapped the arms of the coat loosely around her leg, hoping the bulky material would soak up some of the blood.

"What's your name?" I asked the woman.

She cleared her throat and shook her head, her brow creasing with confusion. Instead, she began a new litany of faint but frantic cries about her family.

"You can tell me later. I'm Hannah."

"Help! My family…!"

"I'm going down into the ravine right now. Stay here. I'll help them. I promise."

Hoping I didn't just make a promise I couldn't keep, I shut the door and tripped my way through the snowdrifts toward the red haloed taillights.

I pulled my phone out of my coat pocket. There usually wasn't cell phone coverage on this road. But, just maybe…

No service.

This wasn't supposed to be happening! I should be at my sister's lodge at the top of the mountain not crawling down a steep embankment to help accident victims!

It wasn't even supposed to be snowing! I'd checked the weather report at least a dozen times: no new snow for the next week. Now it was practically a blizzard!

I took deep breaths, trying to control the panic and adrenaline running through my veins as I half climbed, half slid down the incline. This wasn't me. I'm not the brave sort. In fact, I'm pretty much a wimp!

I was facing the risk of a serious panic attack even before any of this had happened. The rational part of my brain said my fear was ridiculous. The roads were supposed to be clear. I'd driven to Silver Springs many times before. And, I was driving the biggest, meanest, previously-owned SUV an over-protective father could buy for his college-age daughter. Despite my best rationale, my hands were sweating, my heart was beating erratically, and I was still at the bottom of the mountain.

But those symptoms were nothing compared to what I experienced now. When my eyes collided with the blue sedan at the bottom, I wanted to turn around and run. The front of the car was wrapped around a tree. How could anyone survive an accident like this?

The gas station attendant's ramblings from earlier replayed in my head like a bad movie. Something about a tragic accident on this same road five years ago. The family had all died.

Taking a deep breath, I felt renewed determination run through my veins as it hitched a ride on an abundance of adrenaline. I had to do this.

"Hello, can anyone hear me?" I called as I slid the last few feet to the bottom of the ravine. My wrist scraped over some exposed branches on the way down, but the pain didn't register. I called again, louder.

No answer.

I didn't want to do this! I didn't want to see the scene inside the mangled car. I drew in a shaky, hiccuping breath.

Reaching the driver's side door, I shined the flashlight inside. The beam flickered in my shaking hand. I counted three passengers, motionless and unresponsive to the bright light. My stomach flipped as the beam caught blood marring each pale face.

I bent over, hyperventilating and gasping for breath. I couldn't do this! They were probably already dead! I closed my eyes. "Please, God, I can't do this! Help me!"

I released my breath slowly, then quickly swung my flashlight back inside before I lost my nerve.

The driver must be the injured woman's husband. In the back seat were two children. The girl I guessed to be about 7; the boy about 5. Though I put all my weight into it, neither door on the driver's side would budge.

I rushed around to the other side, climbing into the mom's empty seat. Reaching into the back seat and searching for the girl's pulse, I sighed in relief. She was alive—unconscious, but with a strong pulse. I climbed further over the seats and reached for the boy. Another pulse! New energy and determination surged through my veins.

Finally, I leaned over to the dad for a pulse. But I already knew the answer. The front driver's side had taken most of the impact. No one could survive in his position. To my surprise, I felt a slight bump against my finger. It was very faint, but the man was alive… at least for now.

I tried to focus. What could I do? I could drive to the lodge and get my sister, Abby, and her husband, Tom, to come help. We could use the phone at the lodge to call for medical assistance. Then we could get some of the other lodgers, come back and…

I shivered, feeling the freezing cold seep through my coat. It would be too late. I closed my eyes. A sob of fear and frustration caught in my throat. We wouldn't make it back in time. They couldn't survive their injuries or these temperatures for very long. I couldn't leave them. It was all up to me.

I tried not to think. I tried not to feel. I just acted.

The door by the girl opened easily. I unbuckled her seatbelt, took a deep breath, and hoisted her in my arms. She stirred and moaned slightly.

"I've got you. You're going to be alright," I cooed softly as I struggled through the drifts and still-falling snow back up the ravine.

My arms burned with the effort and my labored breathing came in short gasps. Just when I thought I couldn't take another step, I finally reached the SUV. Gently, I placed the girl in the back seat beside her mother.

"Maddie! "The sobbing woman gathered her daughter into her arms.

"I think she's going to be okay," I said, shocked the woman was still conscious. "I have to go back for the others."

Knowing every minute counted, I hurried back to the ravine and climbed into the back seat of the car. I unbuckled the boy's seat belt. He stirred and groaned, his eyes fluttering open.

"Hi, I'm Hannah. I'm going to get you out of here. Where are you hurt?"

"My legs and my head."

The driver's seat was pushed up against him. We both had to work to free his pinned legs. Grunting and groaning, I eventually dragged him out.

Even though this was my second trip back up the ravine, the boy was much easier to carry. Because he was conscious, he wasn't the dead weight his sister had been. As he held on to my neck and buried his face in my hair, I learned his name was Timmy and his favorite thing was fire trucks.

When I put Timmy in the back seat of the SUV, I saw that his mom was struggling to remain conscious.

I faced a moment of indecision. The man might already be dead. It had been tough carrying the kids, and I had no idea how I was going to get a large man up the ravine. Besides, if I took the time to get him, it might be too late for the mom.

Hesitating, I realized it wasn't really a decision. I wouldn't be able to live with myself if I didn't at least try. Having a sudden epiphany, I opened the back of my SUV and removed a tow rope and a tarp.

Since I'd always had a healthy fear of just about every worst case scenario, I took seriously the motto, "Always be prepared." My phobias insured I had well-stocked emergency supplies. I'd just never imagined this situation was one I'd need to prepare for.

When I got to the sedan, I found the man's pulse still barely registering life. It was probably good he was unconscious. He was stuck. I pushed and pulled, trying not to think about any other pain or injuries I may be inflicting. I had to get him out.

He wasn't budging even a little. Panting and sweating, I tried to catch my breath. But it kept coming in short gasps.

I couldn't do it! Great sobs scraped past my throat. I was losing it!

"Please help me!" I prayed desperately, yelling at the top of my lungs.

I crawled over him, kicking and punching his seat like a madwoman.

To my shock, the seat broke. I quickly removed the seat back, using the space to pull the man from behind. His lifeless body finally slid from its cage.

Breathing heavily, I dragged him out of the car and onto the tarp I had positioned. I wrapped the tarp around him and tied one end of the rope under his arms. Grabbing the other end, I pulled. The tarp slid across the snow.

Even with the tarp, the man was dead weight. I'd heard that adrenaline had been known to give a person superhuman strength. That and some divine assistance is the only explanation I have for how my 5'6'' frame was able to drag that man uphill out of the ravine and then lift him into the rear of the SUV.

Finally back inside my SUV, my frozen fingers gripped the steering wheel in terror as I drove through the snow. The woman was unconscious now. I had to get to the lodge.

Timmy was the only one conscious. He was amazingly calm. We talked about his Christmas list. From Hot Wheels to remote controls, Timmy wanted such variety of cars and trucks that Santa would have his work cut out for him.

My breath caught with relief as I saw the lights of Silver Springs through the swirling snow. Stopping in front of the lodge, I jumped out. Frantic, I yelled, banging my fists on the front door. An elderly man I didn't recognize opened it.

I don't remember what I told him. Everything I said seemed like gibberish in my head, but he apparently understood.

"Go get McAllister!" he called to an older woman near the stairs. He then turned and explained to me that a doctor was vacationing at the lodge.

The older man and two others gently carried each person to the large living room where the doctor known as McAllister was putting on a pair of rubber gloves.

Scanning the patients, he called to the man from the door. "George, we're going to need a helicopter."

My eyes met the doctor's blue-green ones and held. He was a lot younger than I had expected, with a strong face and dark, wavy blond hair to go with those rather incredible eyes.

"Who's injured the worst?" he asked.

"The man," I replied. "I'm not sure he's still alive. His pulse was very weak even before I pulled him out of the wreck."

Dr. McAllister's eyes shot back to me, sizing me up. Obviously having questions, he said instead, "I need some help."

Maybe he assumed I had some medical training. Then again, maybe I was just the best choice of assistants. The other three guys in the room didn't look like they would be able to tell the difference between a pair of tweezers and a chainsaw.

I followed Dr. McAllister as he checked each patient. I don't remember what he did. I was in a daze, simply following his orders.

The loud chopping of a helicopter broke the hush of the room. Paramedics rushed in with gurneys and quickly transferred the family to the waiting helicopter. As the lights and sounds faded away, Dr. McAlister took my hand, led me to a couch in front of the fire, and placed a mug of hot cocoa in my stiff fingers.

He sat down beside me, his gaze concerned. "I haven't even asked if you are hurt."

"No. Just cold."

He wrapped a blanket around me, saying, "Can you tell me what happened?"

Almost like a recitation, I recounted every detail, but it was like I was talking about someone else. I felt nothing.

When I finished, I asked softly, "Are they going to be alright, Dr. McAlister?" I vaguely noticed that my hands around the mug had begun shaking.

He winced. Seeing my cocoa was about to slosh out of my hands, he took the mug, put it on the coffee table, and held my cold hands in his warm ones.

His eyes met mine. "Call me Seth. And I'm not really a doctor, not yet anyway. I'm in medical school. George is an old friend who tends to exaggerate my accomplishments and ignore my faults."

"I'm Hannah."

Knowing I was still waiting for an answer, he sighed. "I think the kids are going to be fine. I'm not sure about the mom. She's lost a lot of blood. I don't think the dad will make it. They'll do everything possible, but his chances are very slim."

I appreciated his honesty. "I don't know why my hands are shaking," I murmured. Thinking back to what I had done, I felt a burning behind my eyes. "I had to do a lot of maneuvering to get the man out of the car. It was really rough. Maybe I hurt him more."

I whispered. "Do you think he'll die because of something I did?"

Warm tears rolled down my face. Seth took my face in his gentle hands, lifting my chin so our eyes met.

"Hannah, none of those people would have made it without you. Do you understand? They would have all died. You told me, but I still don't understand how you did it. I do know that you saved them." His thumb massaged my cheek. "I don't think I've ever met a woman who was so strong and brave."

I let out an almost hysterical giggle. "I'm not brave at all. If you only knew. My own shadow scares me regularly!"

"You did what had to be done even though you were afraid. I call that bravery."

Seeing his honest face looking at me with such admiration, I lost it. The shaking hands turned into full body convulsions. The hysterical giggling transformed into heaving sobs. I couldn't catch my breath. My throat, eyes, and chest burned, but I was so cold. I relived yet again every last detail of the night. But this time, I felt everything.

Seth held me close, caressing my hair, wiping my tears, whispering words of comfort. His lips traced gentle kisses across my forehead. While this would normally be a strange intimacy with someone I just met, with Seth it felt right. Comforting.

Eventually I felt the warmth of his strong arms seep through the cold. My sobs lessened as my body relaxed. I clung to Seth. I felt a blessed numbness as warmth stole over me. My eyelids grew impossibly heavy.

As if in a dream, I felt myself being carried, floating up the stairs until I was laid gently upon a soft bed. Seth covered me with a blanket. I tried to speak, but I couldn't remember any words. I felt a gentle kiss on my forehead and a whispered, "Good night." My last memory was of those blue-green eyes and a feather-light touch on my face.

If you enjoyed this preview, YESTERDAY, and other books by Amanda Tru may be purchased from the same online store where you purchased this book. Happy reading!

About the Author

Amanda loves to write exciting books with plenty of unexpected twists. She figures she loses so much sleep writing the things, it's only fair she makes readers lose sleep with books they can't put down!

Amanda has always loved reading, and writing books has been a lifelong dream. A vivid imagination helps her write captivating stories in a wide variety of genres. Her current book list includes everything from holiday romances, to action-packed suspense, to a Christian time travel / romance series.

Amanda is a former elementary school teacher who now spends her days being mommy to three little boys and her nights furiously writing. Amanda and her family live in a small Idaho town where the number of cows outnumbers the number of people.

You can find Amanda Tru on Facebook or at her website! She loves hearing from readers!
Facebook:
https://www.facebook.com/amandatru.author
Website:
http://www.amandatru.blogspot.com
Email:
truamanda@gmail.com